THE QUOTABLE
SANDMAN ™

THE QUOTABLE SANDMAN. Published by DC Comics, 1700 Broadway, New York, NY 10019. Compilation © 2000 DC Comics. All rights reserved. VERTIGO, all characters featured in this issue, the distinctive likenesses thereof and all related indicia are trademarks of DC Comics. The characters, names and incidents mentioned in this magazine are entirely fictional.

DC Comics. A division of Warner Bros. — A Time Warner Entertainment Company.

Printed in China. First printing.
ISBN 1-56389-747-4

THE QUOTABLE SANDMAN™

Memorable lines from the acclaimed series

Neil Gaiman

Illustrations by a remarkable ensemble of artists

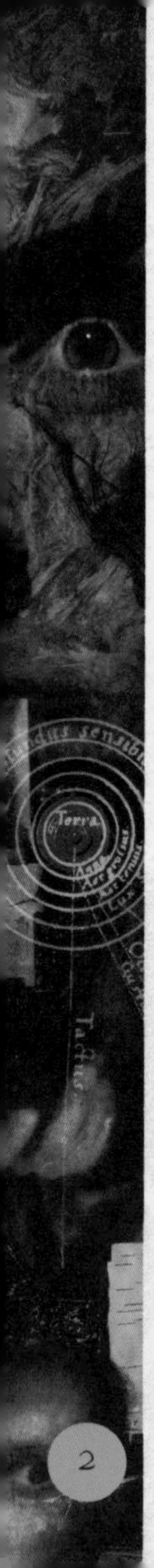
Terra

Things need not have happened to be true.
Tales and dreams are the shadow-truths
that will endure when mere facts
are dust and ashes,
and forgot.

—Dream

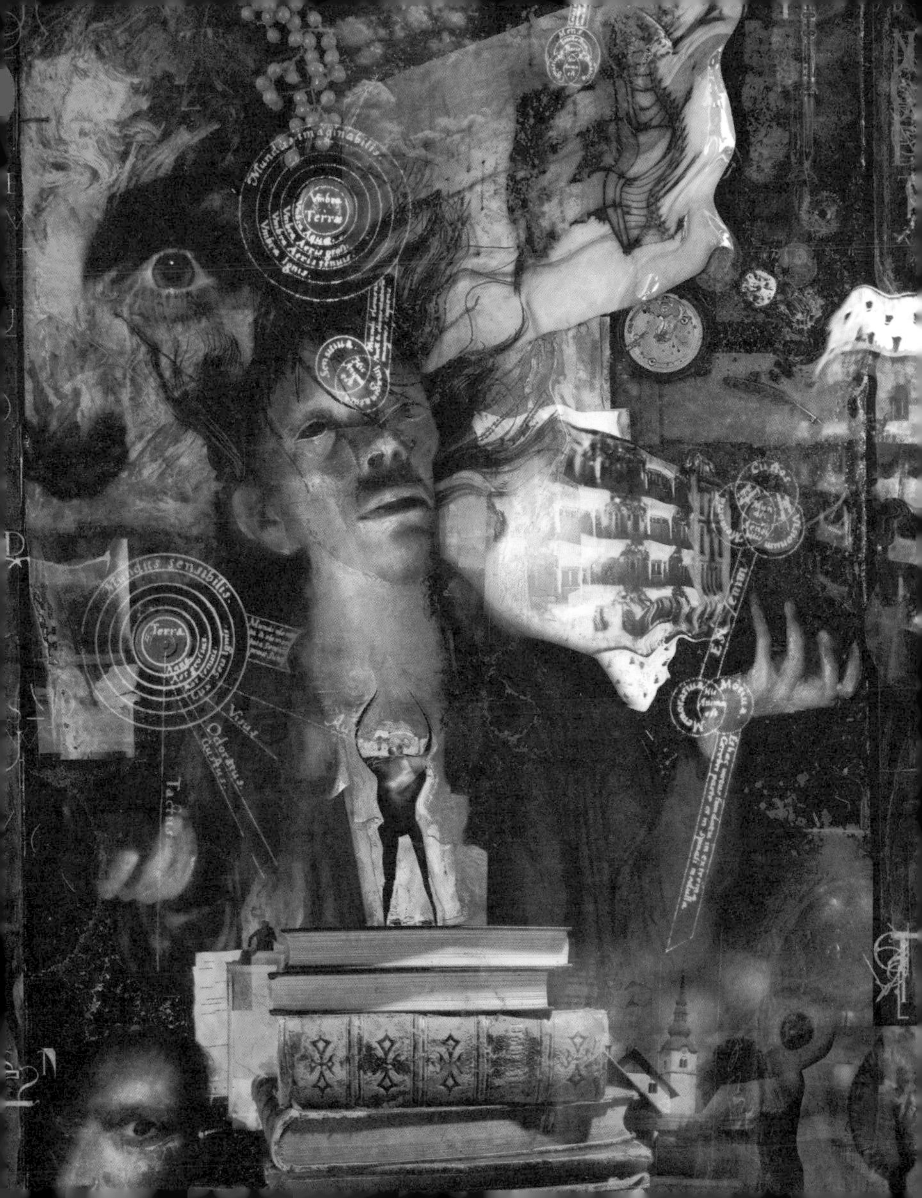

Mundus imaginabilis
Umbra Terræ
Umbra Aquæ
Umbra Aeris grossi
Umbra Aeris tenuis
Umbra Ignis
Mundus sensibilis
Terra
Visus
Odoratus
Tactus

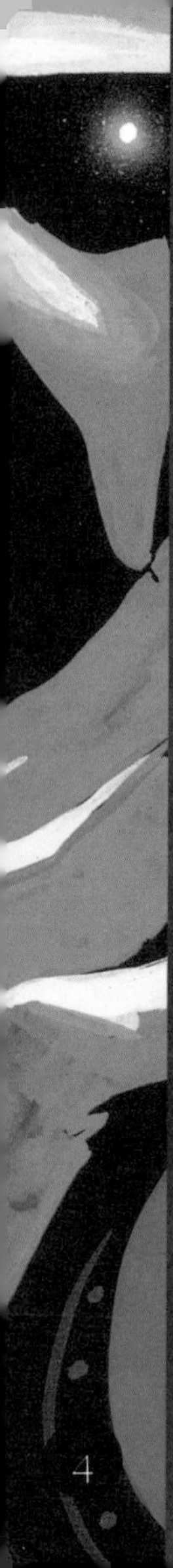

So what I want to know is, when I'm asleep, do
I really remember how to fly?

And forget how when I wake up?
Or am I just dreaming I can fly?

When you dream,
sometimes you remember.
When you wake,
you always forget.

—Chloe Russell to Dream

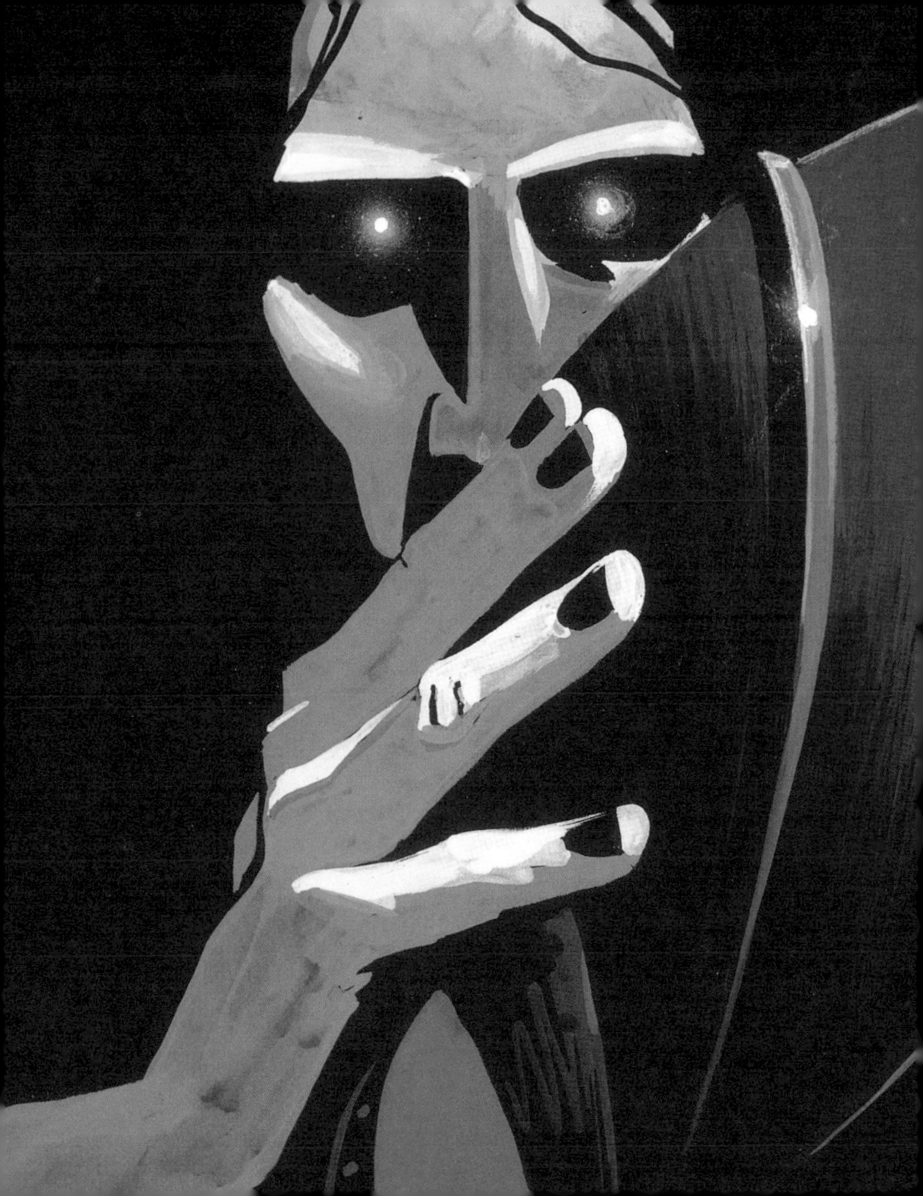

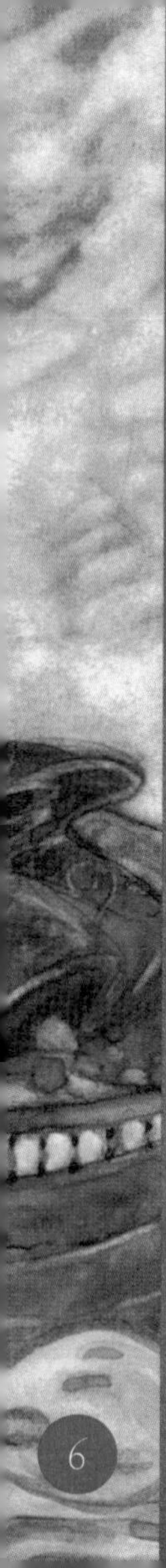

Dream accumulates names to himself like others make friends; but he permits himself few friends.

If he is closest to anyone, it is to his elder sister, whom he sees but rarely.

He heard long ago, in a dream, that one day in every century Death takes on mortal flesh, better to comprehend what the lives she takes must feel like, to taste the bitter tang of mortality: that this is the price she must pay for being the divider of the living from all that has gone before, all that must come after.

— Narrator

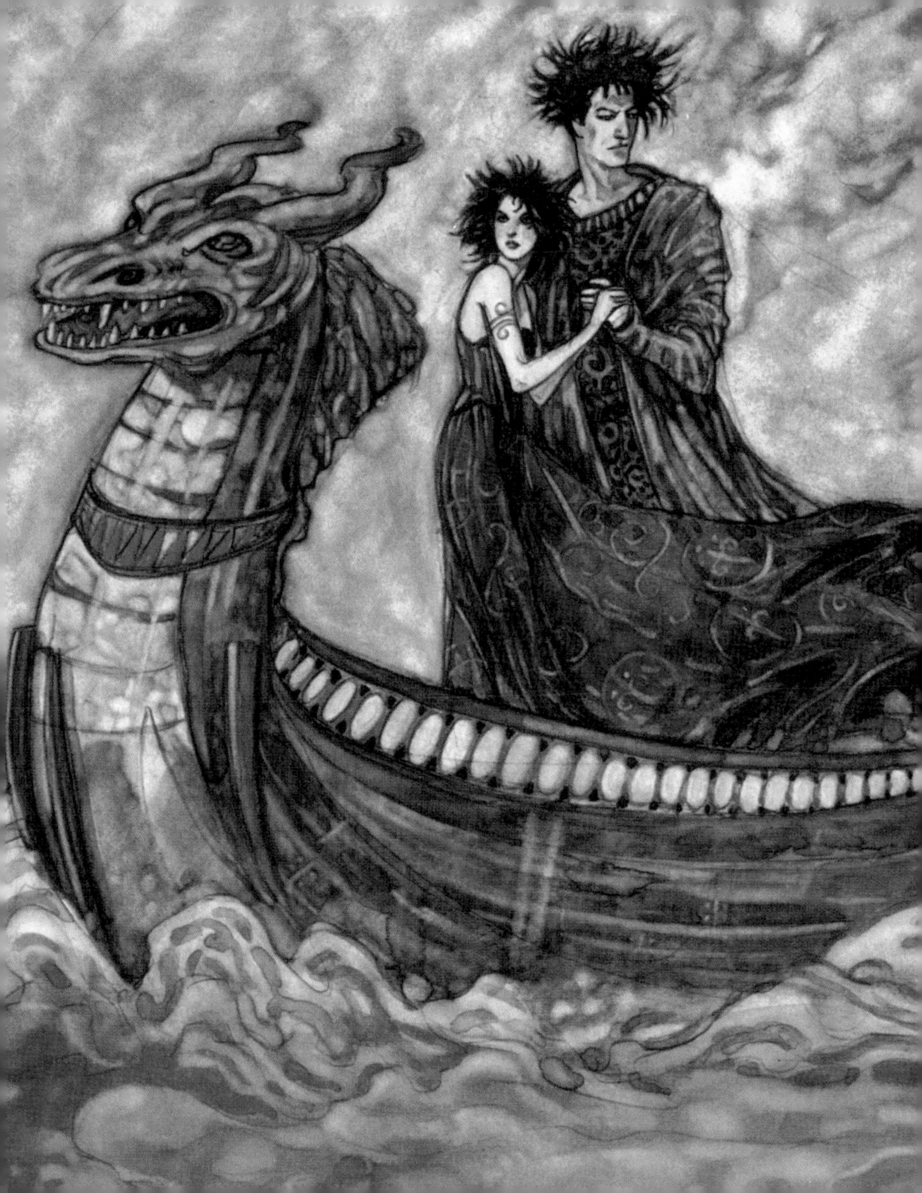

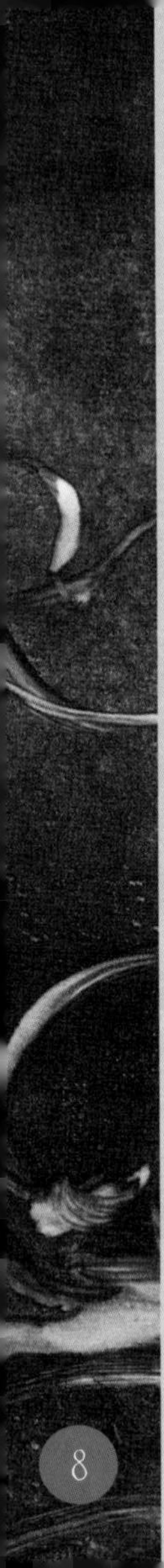

Sometimes we can choose
the path we follow.
Sometimes our choices
are made for us.

And sometimes we have
no choice at all.

—Dream

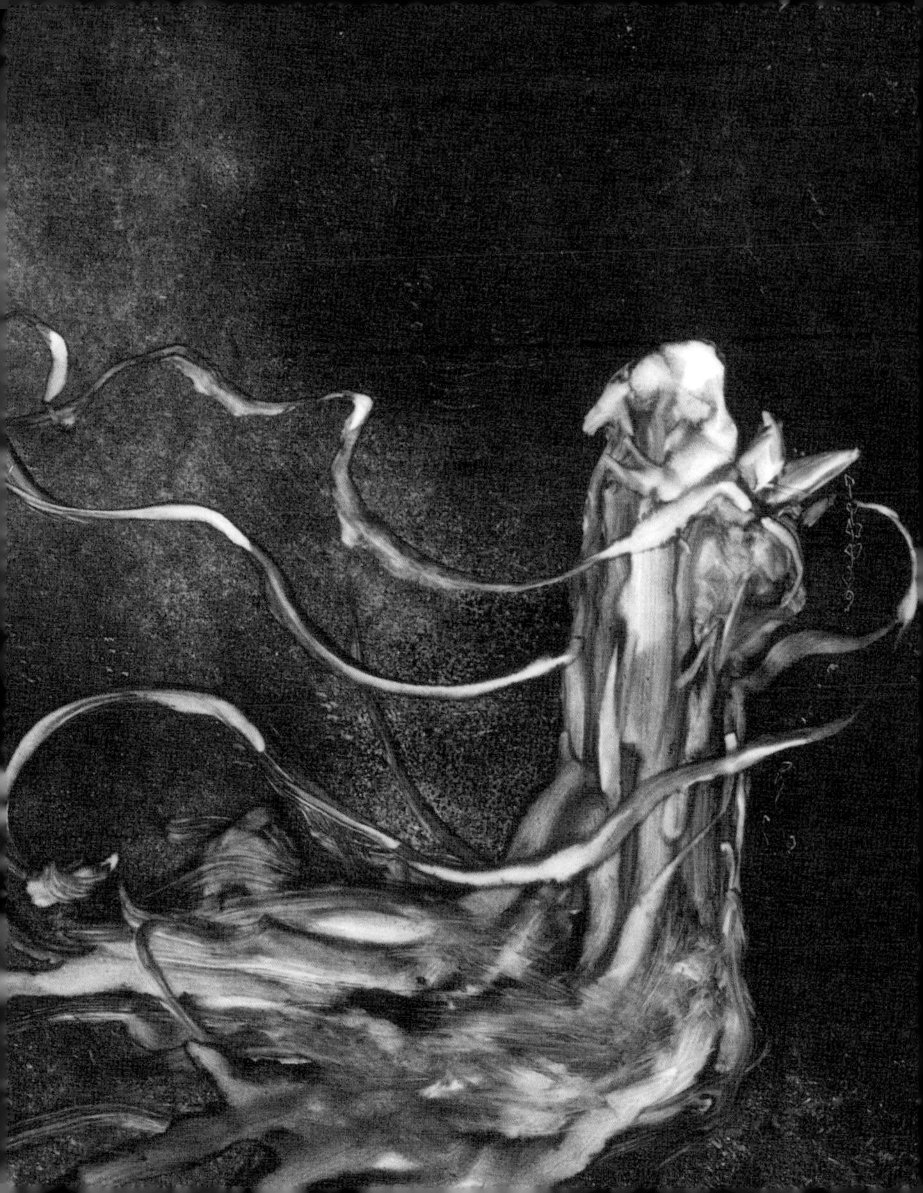

Destinations

are often

a surprise

to the

destined.

— Thessaly

If you do not climb,
    you will not fall. This is true.
But is it that bad to fail,
    that hard to fall?

    — Dream

Sometimes you wake up.
    Sometimes the fall kills you.

And sometimes,
    when you fall,
        you fly.

    — Todd Faber

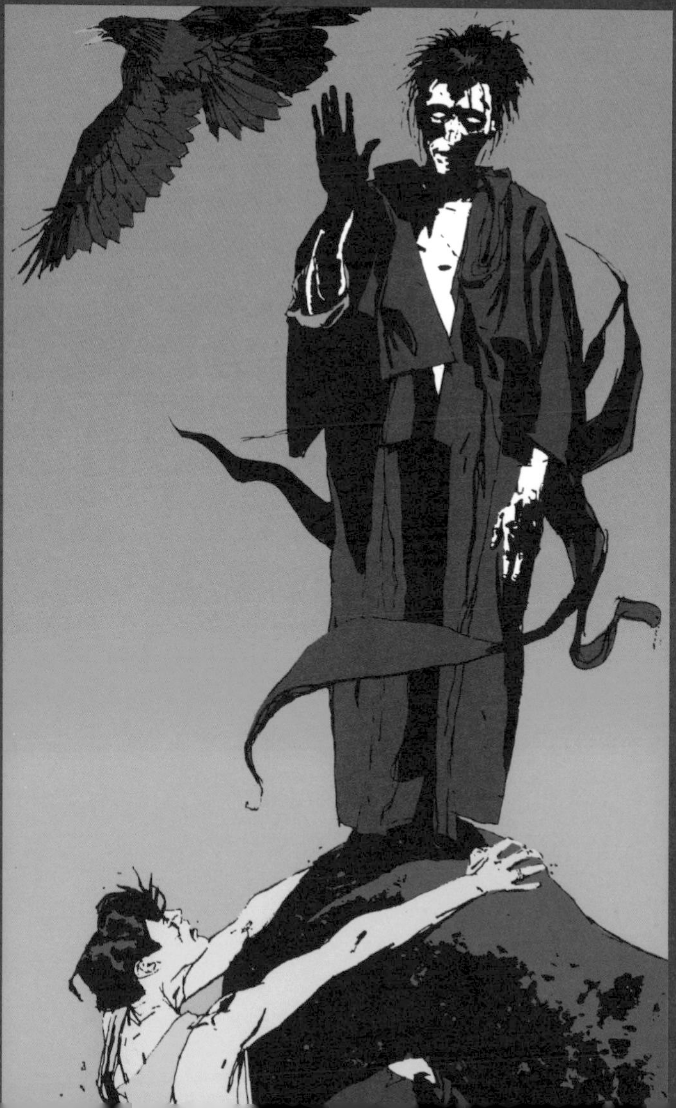

Say, whoever you are,
you know what Freud said
about dreams about
flying?

He said it means you
are really dreaming about
having sex.

Really?
Then tell me, what does it mean
when you dream about having sex?

— Rose Walker to Dream

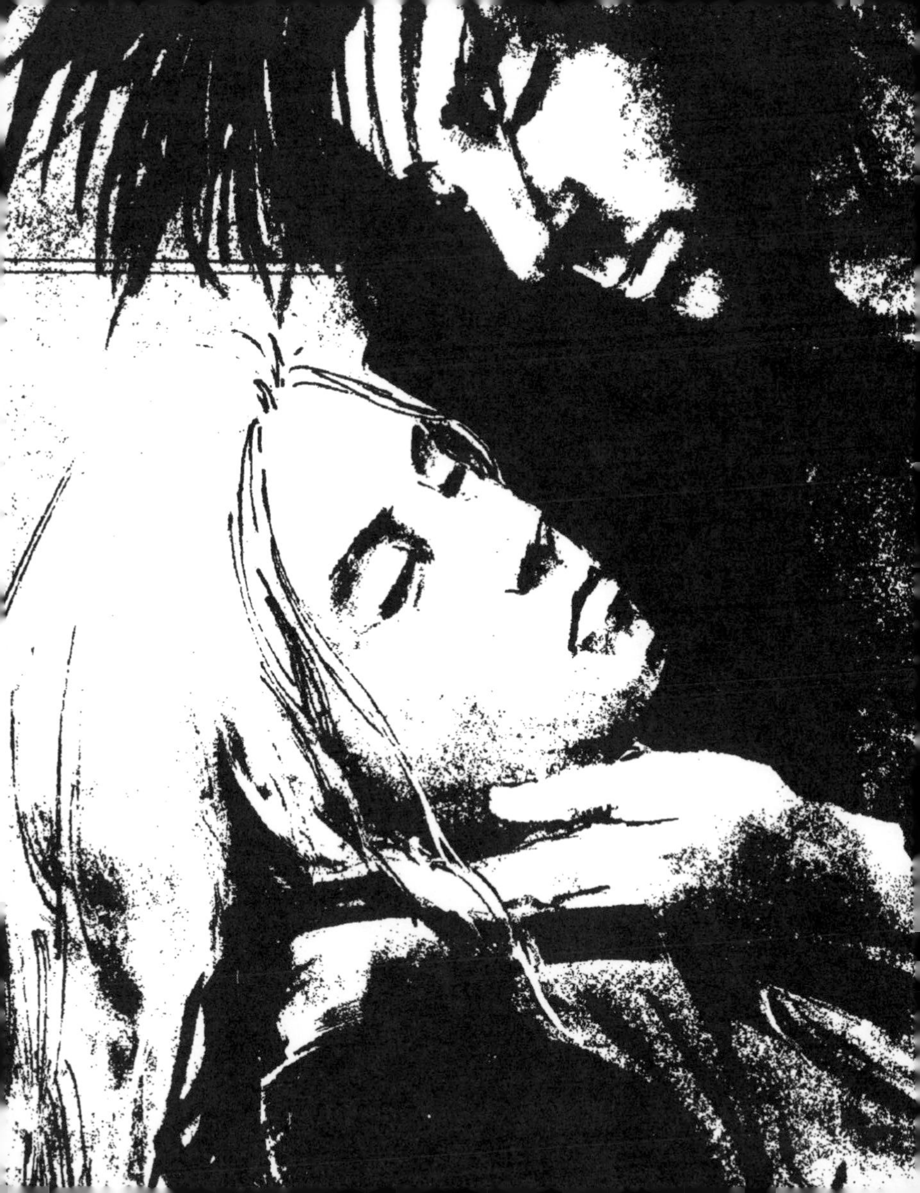

It's astonishing

how much trouble

one can get

oneself into,

if one works at it.

— Destruction

Have you ever spent days
   and days
      and days
   making up flavors of ice cream
      that no one's ever eaten before?

Like chicken and telephone ice cream? ....
Green mouse ice cream was the worst.

                    I didn't like that at all.

                         — Delirium

18

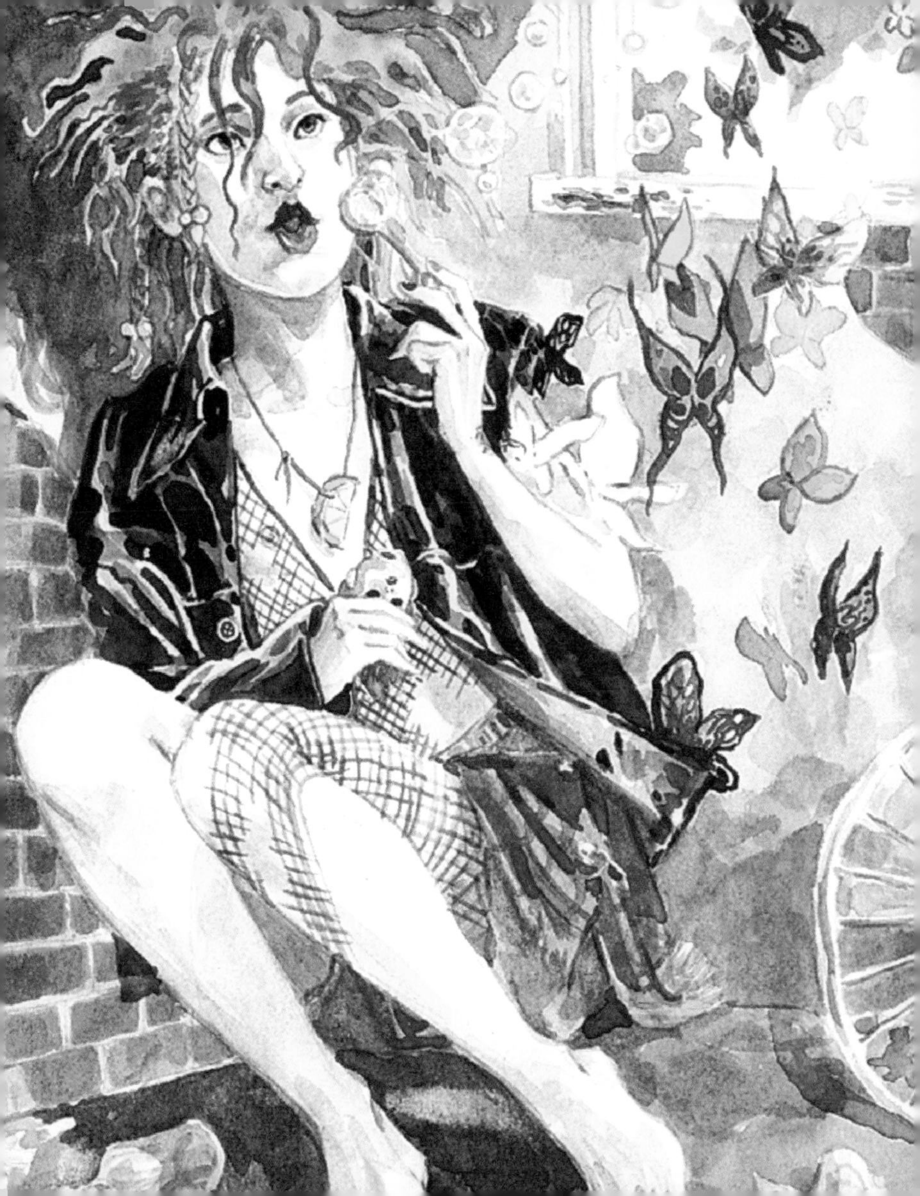

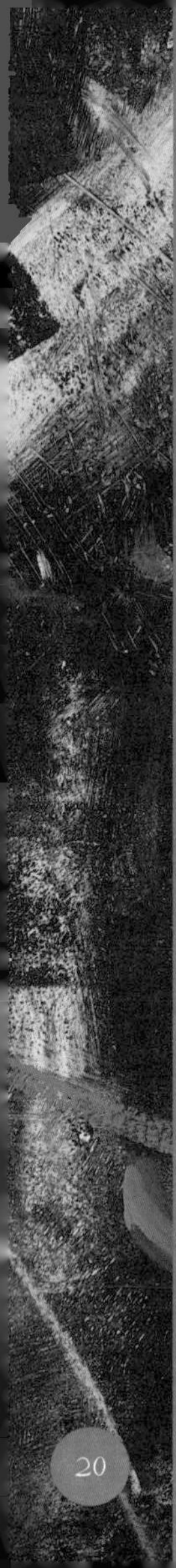

Is there any person in the world
who does not dream?
Who does not contain within them
worlds unimagined?

— Narrator

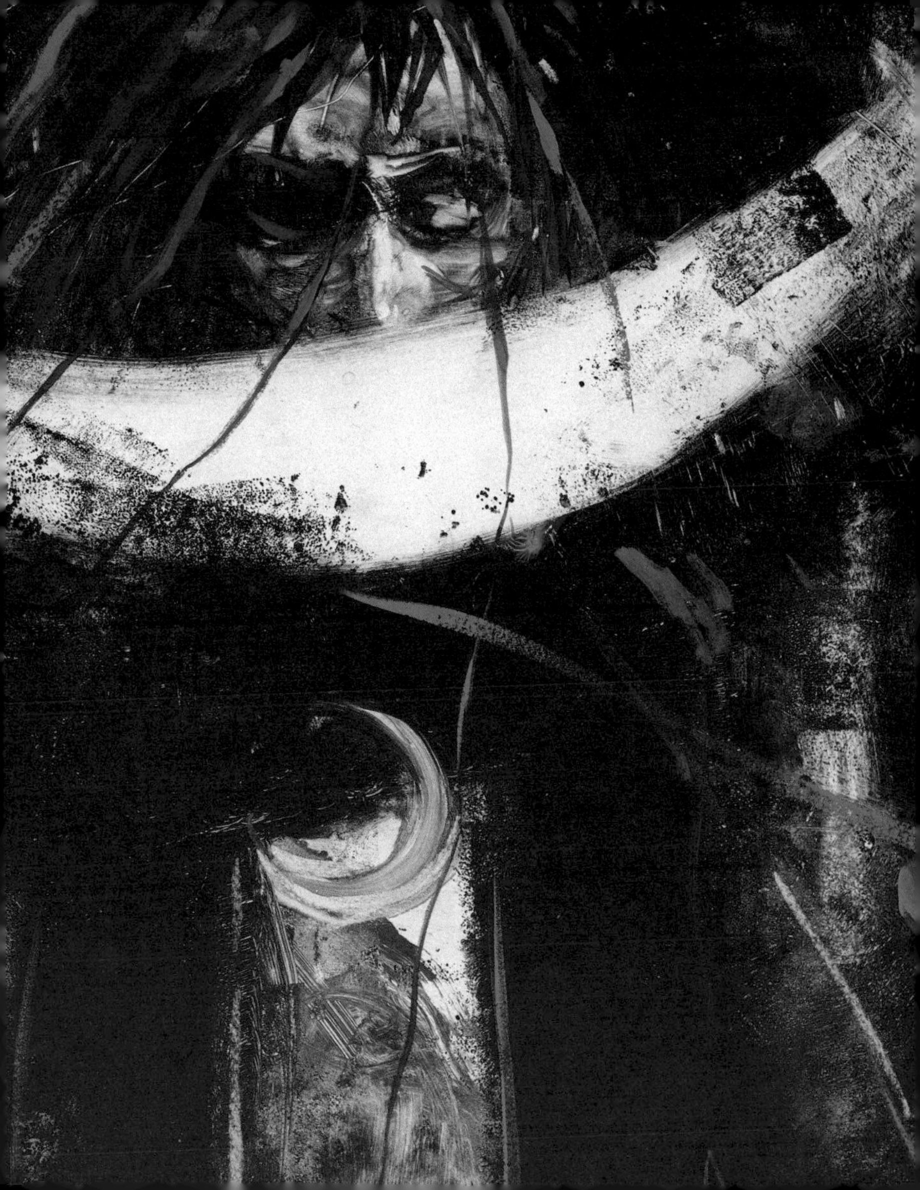

Perhaps a city is a living thing. Each city has its own personality, after all.

Los Angeles is not Vienna. London is not Moscow. Chicago is not Paris. Each city is a collection of lives and buildings and it has its own personality.

So, if a city has a personality, maybe it also has a soul. Maybe it dreams.

I do not fear cities sleeping, stretched out unconscious around their rivers and estuaries, like cats in the moonlight. Sleeping cities are tame and harmless things.

What I fear . . . is that one day the cities will waken. That one day the cities will rise.

— Old Man

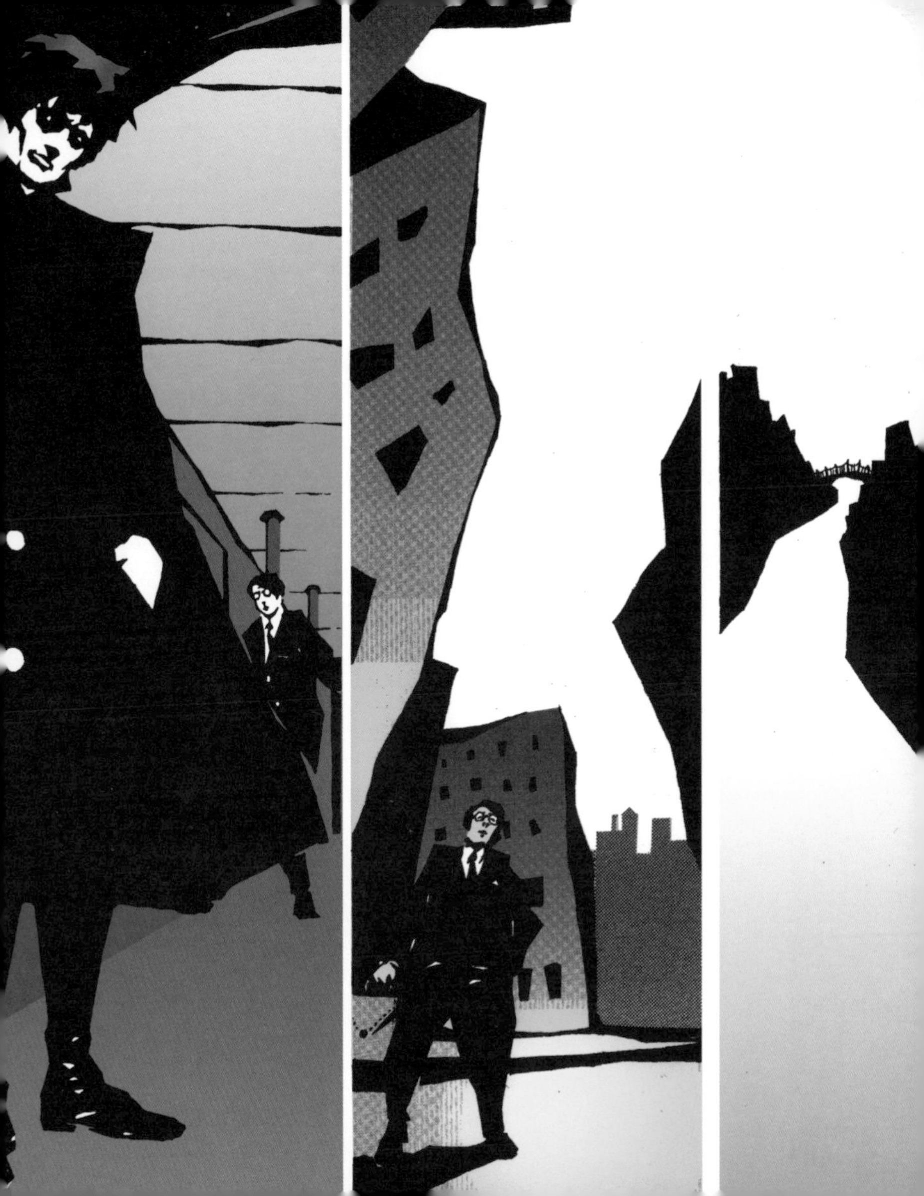

It is a fool's prerogative
to utter truths
that no one else will speak.

—Dream

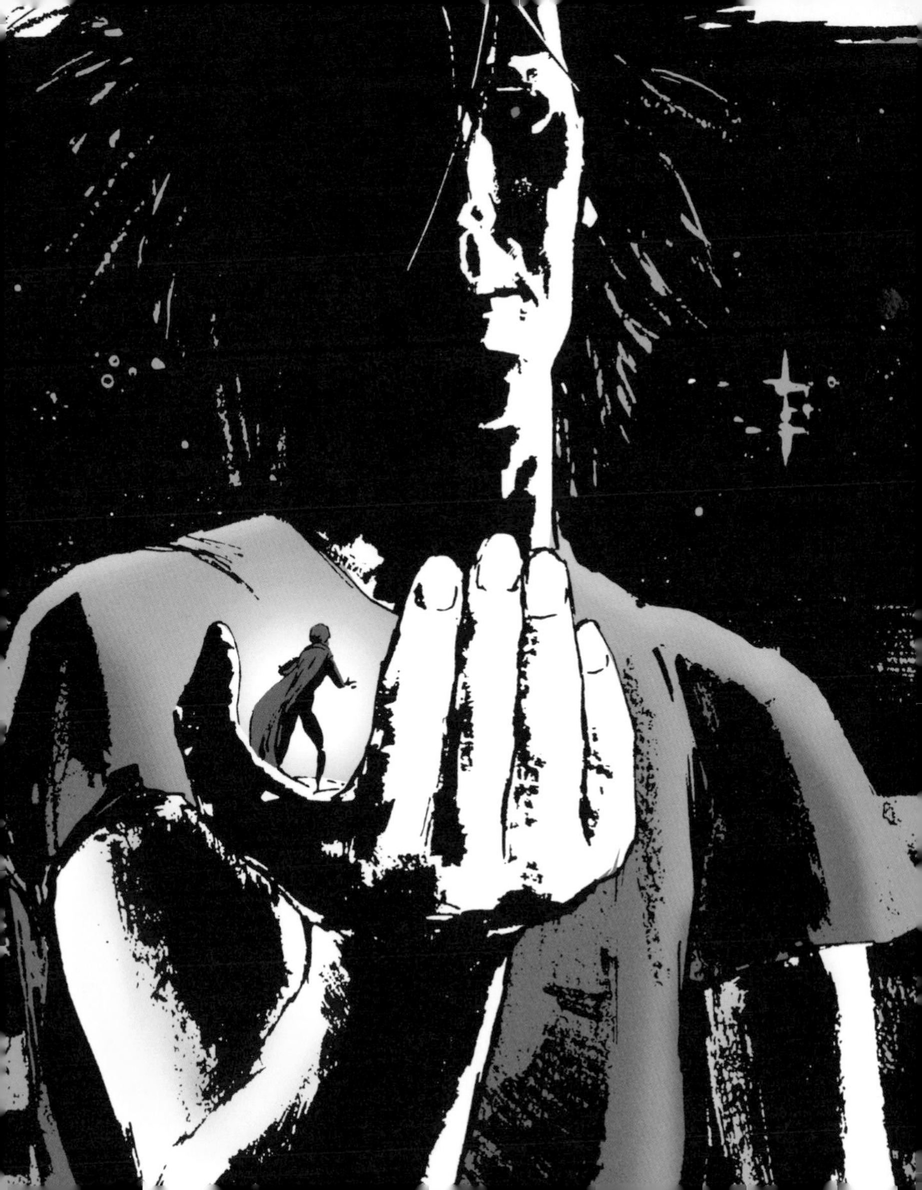

You are utterly the stupidest, most self-centered, appallingest excuse for an anthropomorphic personification on this or any other plane!

— Death

"The Devil made me do it."

I have never made one of them do anything. They live their own tiny lives.

I do not live their lives for them.

— Lucifer

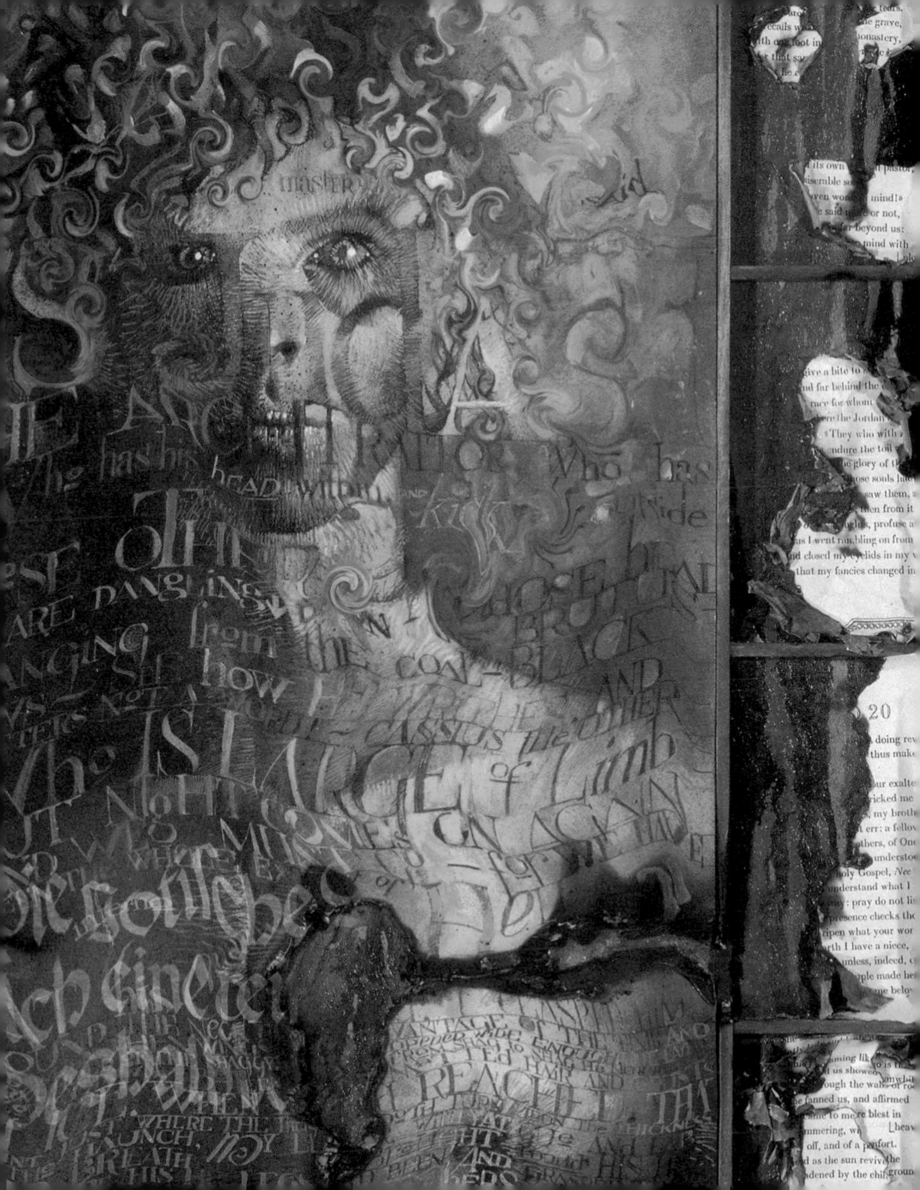

master
Who has
from
how
of Limb
REACHED
20

Little one, I would like to
see anyone — prophet,
king or god —
persuade a thousand
cats to do anything
at the same time.

— Orange Cat

Some things are changeless.

People love, and die, they dream,

destroy, despair, go mad. They fulfill their destinies,

live out the course of their lives.

We fulfill our function, as they

fulfill theirs. That will not change.

— Despair

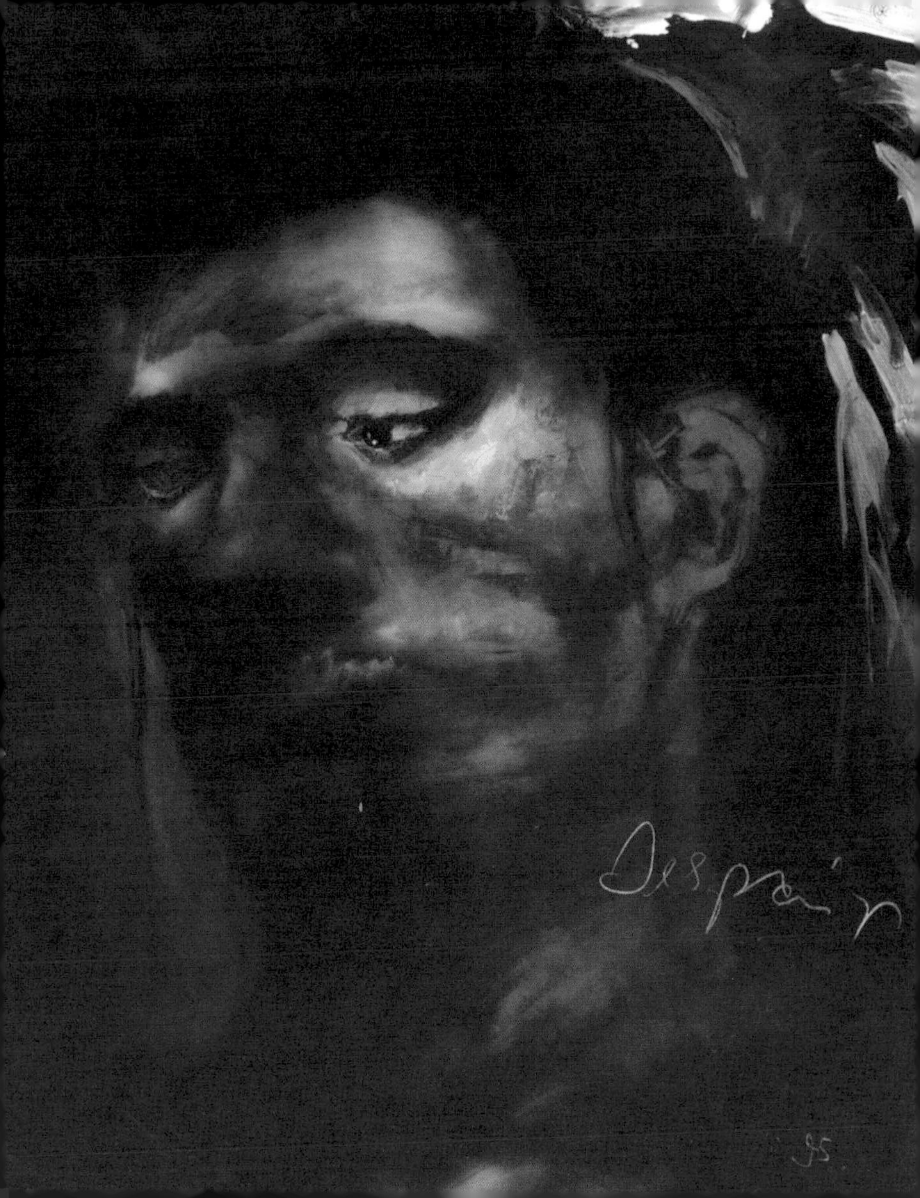
Despair
95.

But he did not understand the price.

Mortals never do.

They only see the prize, their heart's

desire, their dream...

But the price of getting

what you want

is getting what you once wanted.

—Dream

34

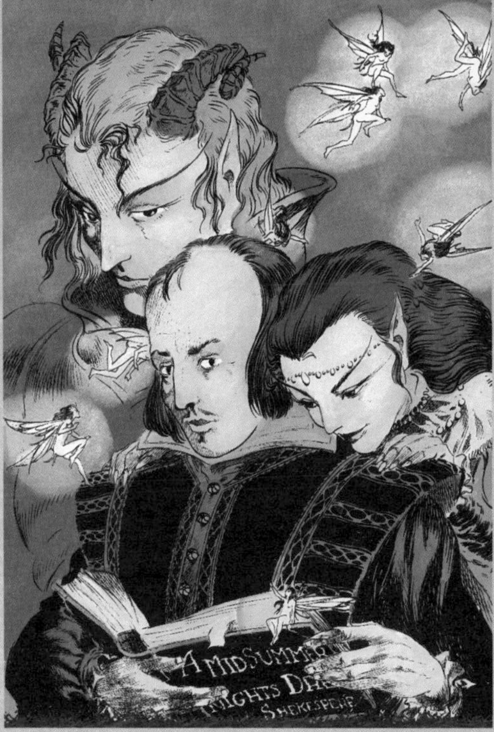
A MIDSUMM
IGHTS DR

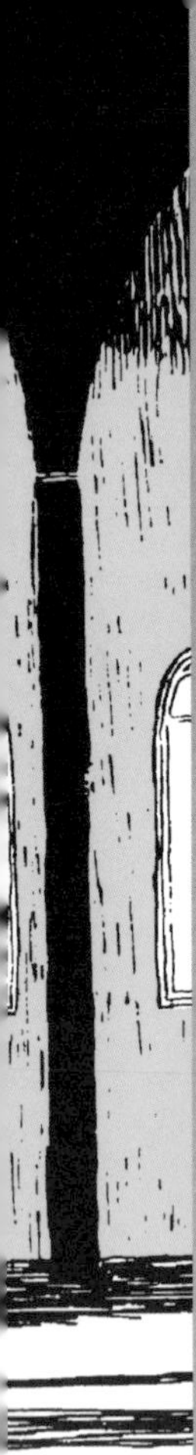

You should have gone to the funeral.

Why?

To say goodbye.

I have not yet said goodbye to Eurydice.

You should. You are mortal:
it is the mortal way. You attend the
funeral, you bid the dead farewell. You grieve. Then
you continue with your life. And at times the fact of
her absence will hit you like a blow to the chest, and
you will weep. But this will happen less and less
as time goes on. She is dead.

You are alive. So live.

— Dream to his son Orpheus

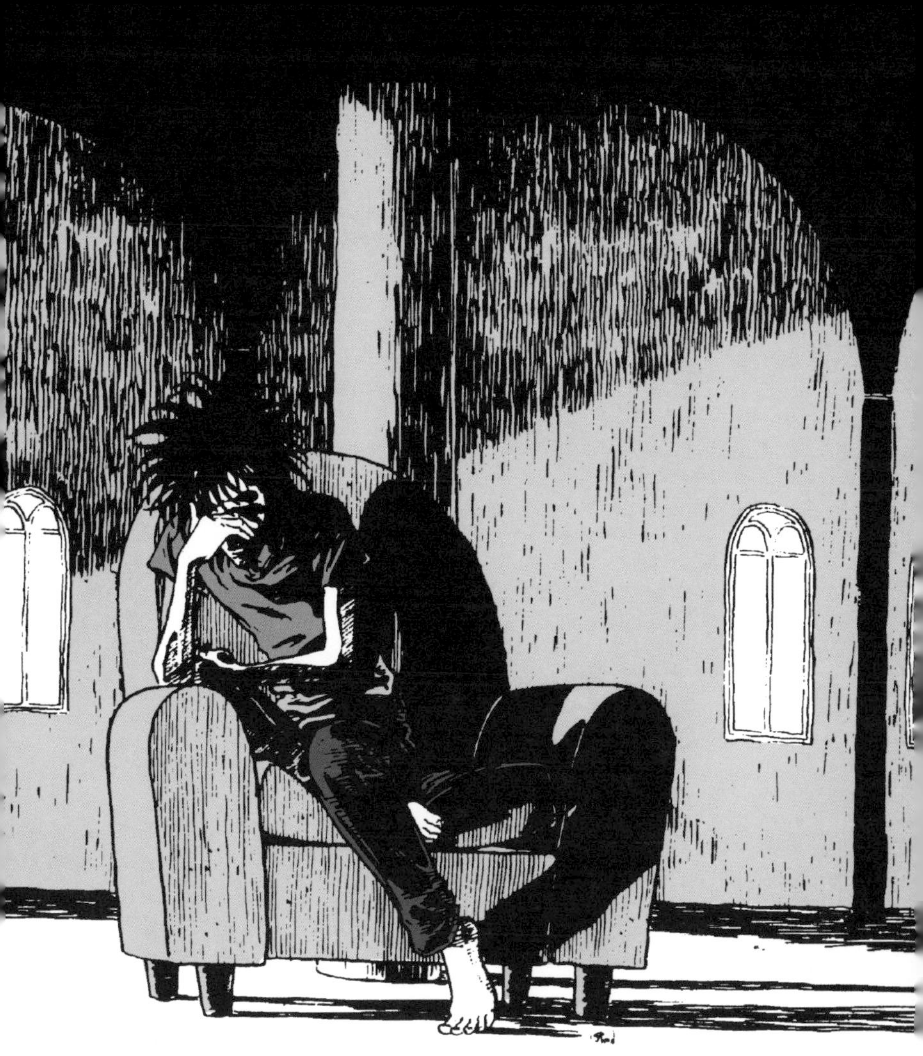

I can pretend that things last.

I can pretend that lives last longer than

moments. Gods come, and gods go.

Mortals flicker and flash and fade.

Worlds don't last; and stars and galaxies

are transient, fleeting things that twinkle like fire-

flies and vanish into cold and dust.

But I can pretend.

— Destruction

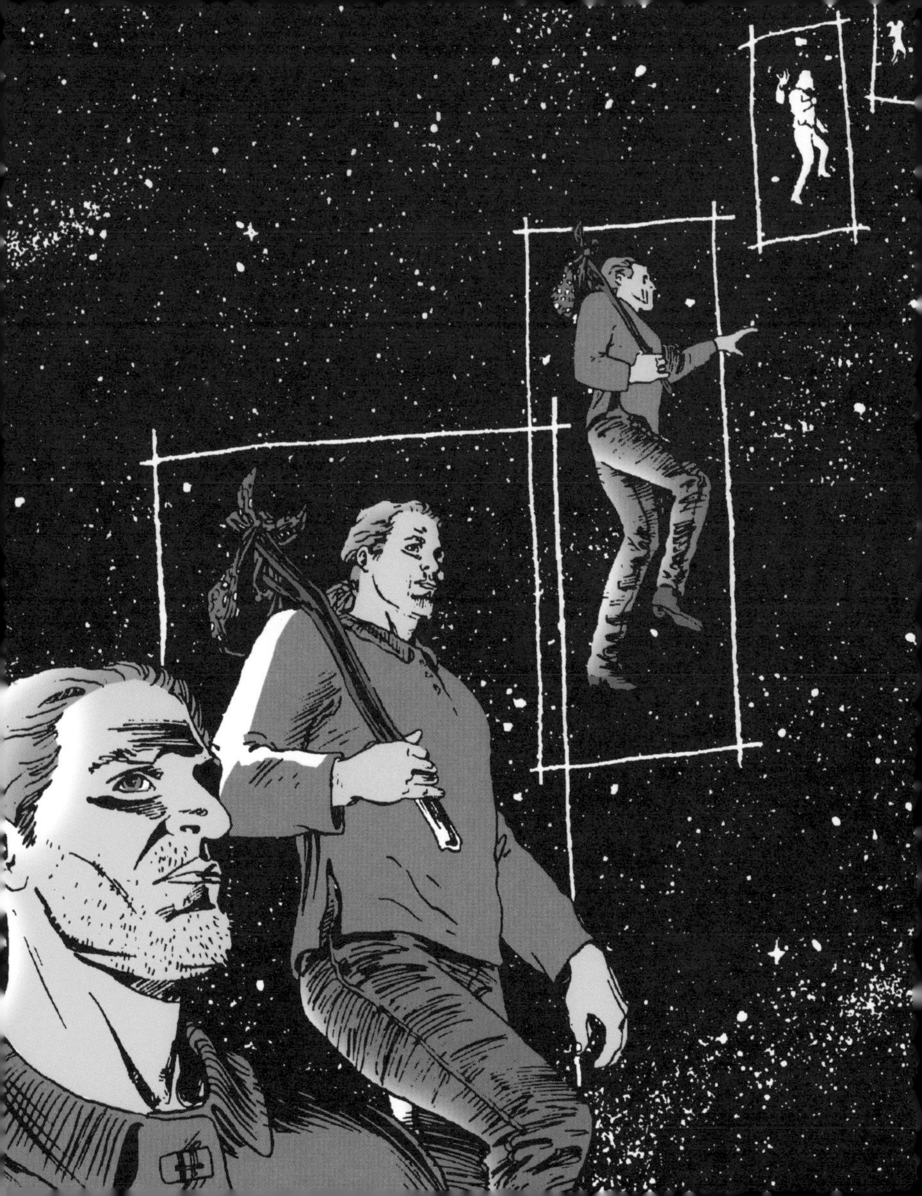

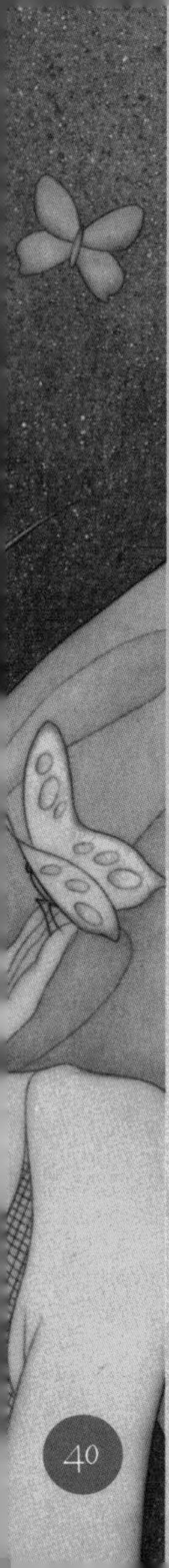

Our existence deforms the universe.
That's responsibility.

— Delirium

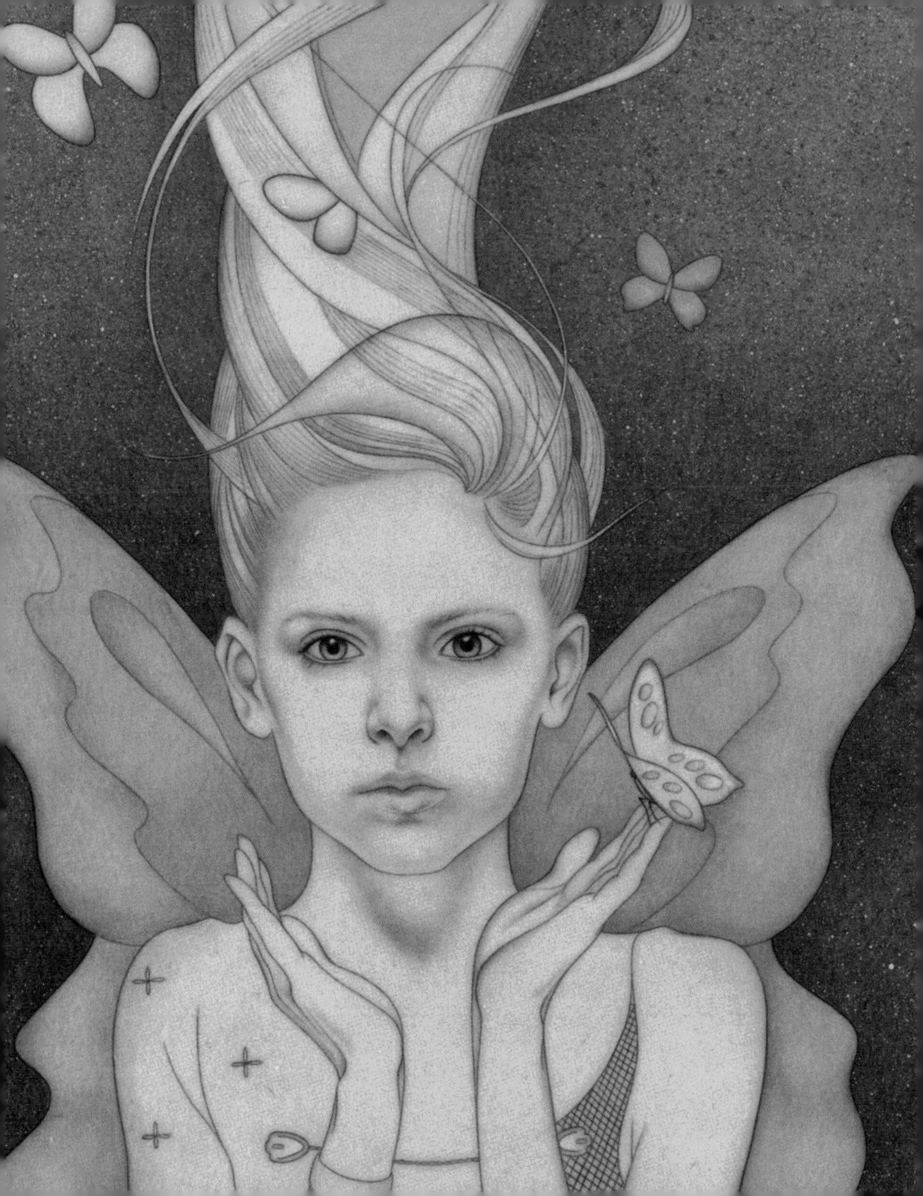

We do what we do because of who we are. If we did otherwise, we would not be ourselves.

—Dream

When the first living thing existed,
     I was there waiting.

When the last living thing dies,
     my job will be finished.

I'll put the chairs on the tables,
     turn out the lights,
          and lock the universe
              behind me as I leave.

— Death

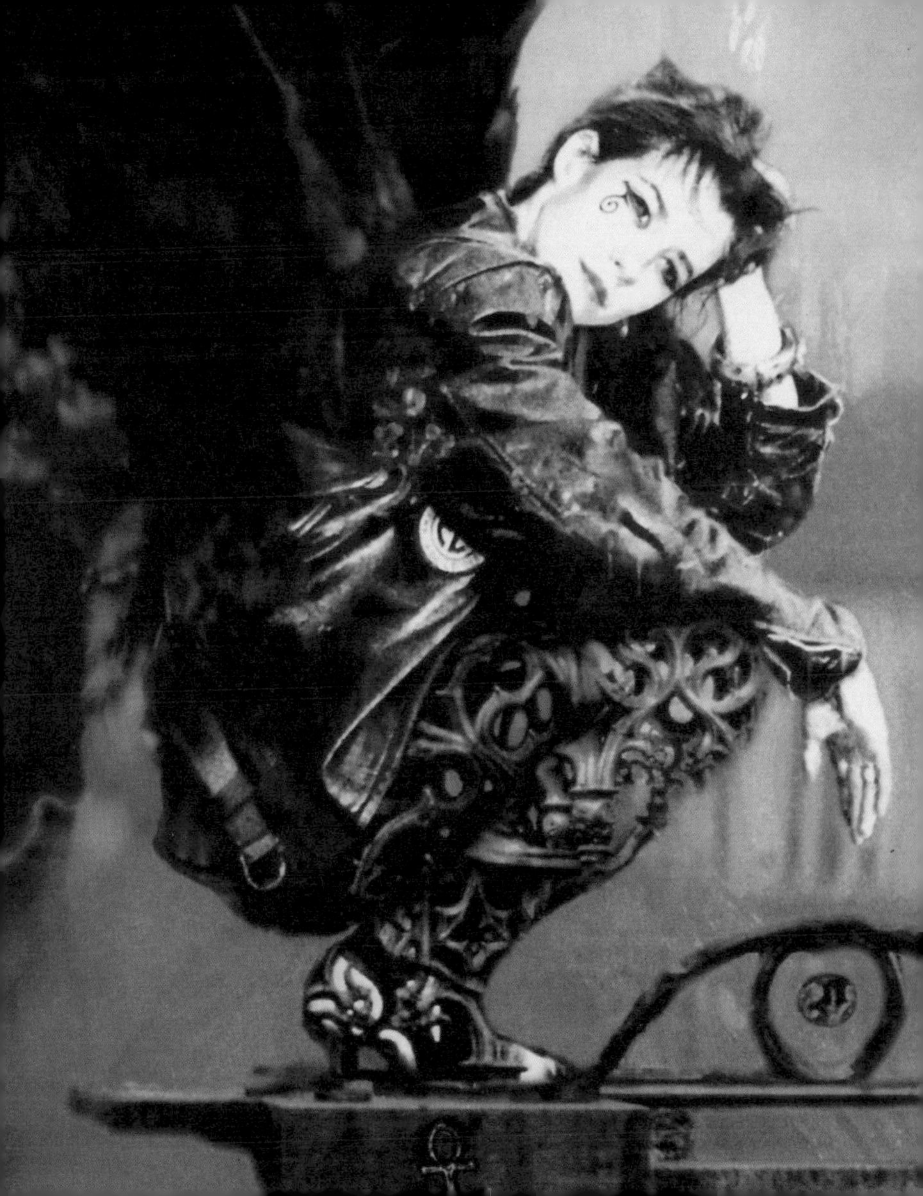

Our sister defines life,

just as Despair defines hope,

or Desire defines hatred,

or as Destiny defines freedom.

— Destruction

46

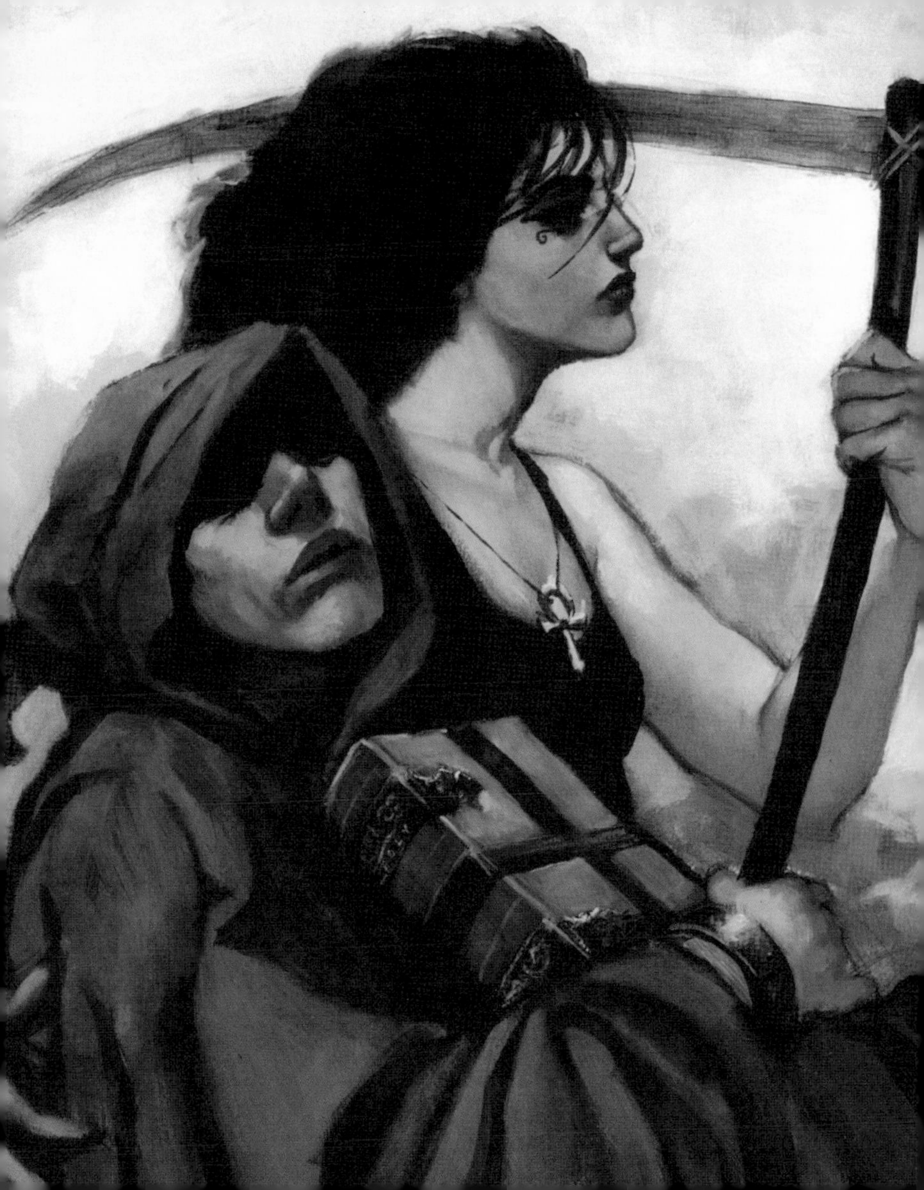

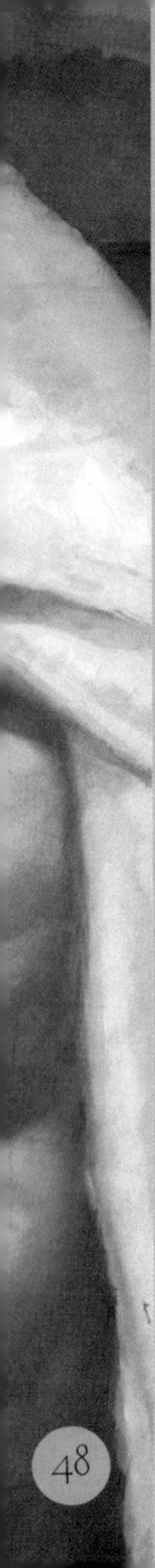

Never a possession, always the possessor, with skin as pale as smoke, and eyes tawny and sharp as yellow wine:

Desire is everything you've ever wanted. Whoever you are. Whatever you are.

Everything.

— Narrator

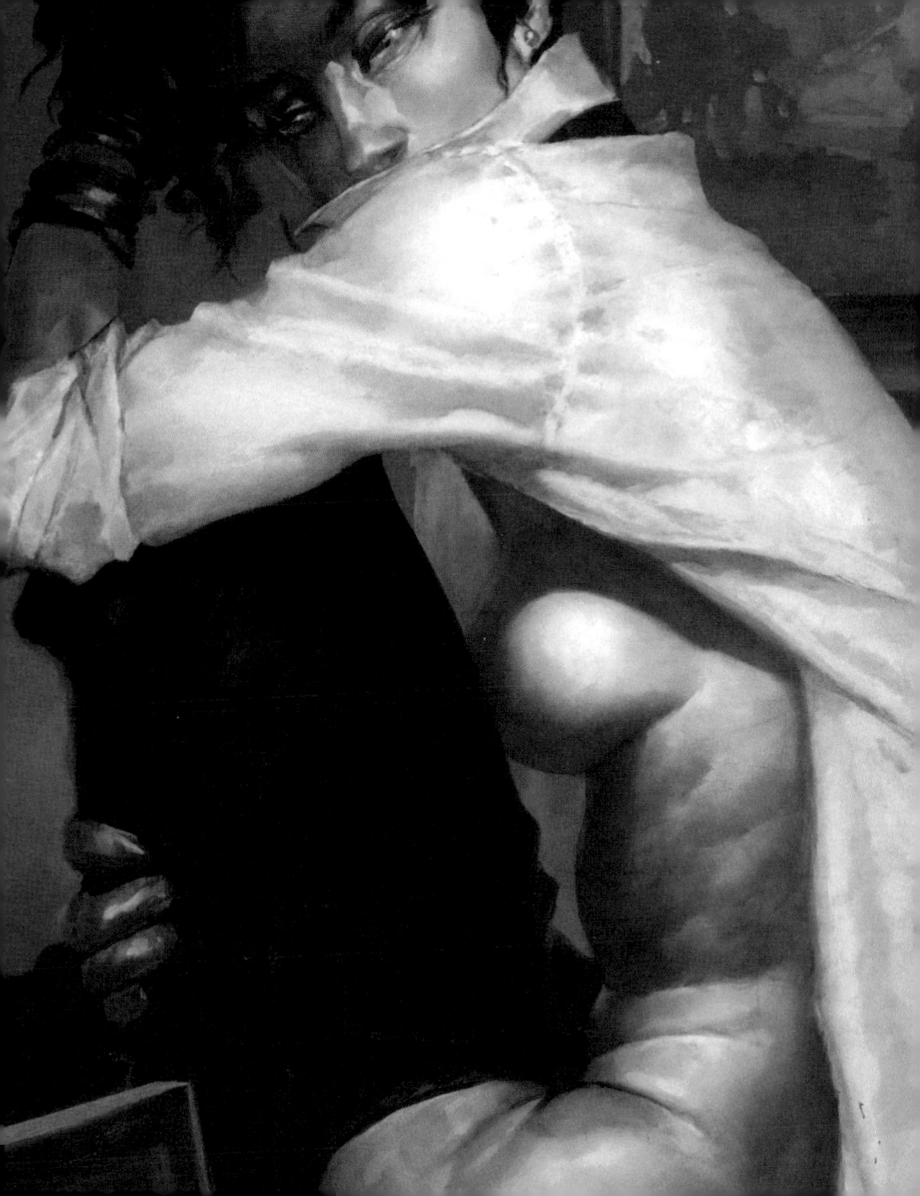

Nah. He enjoys it. I mean, hell, it's a pose. Y'know? He spends a coupla months hanging out with a new broad. Then one day the magic's worn off, and he goes back to work, and she takes a hike. Phhht. Now, guys like me, ordinary Joes, we just shrug our shoulders, say, hey, that's life, flick it if you can't take a joke. Not him. Oh no. He's gotta be the tragic figure standing out in the rain, mourning the loss of his beloved. So down comes the rain, right on cue. In the meantime everybody gets dreams fulla existential angst and wakes up feeling like hell. And we all get wet.

— Mervyn Pumpkinhead

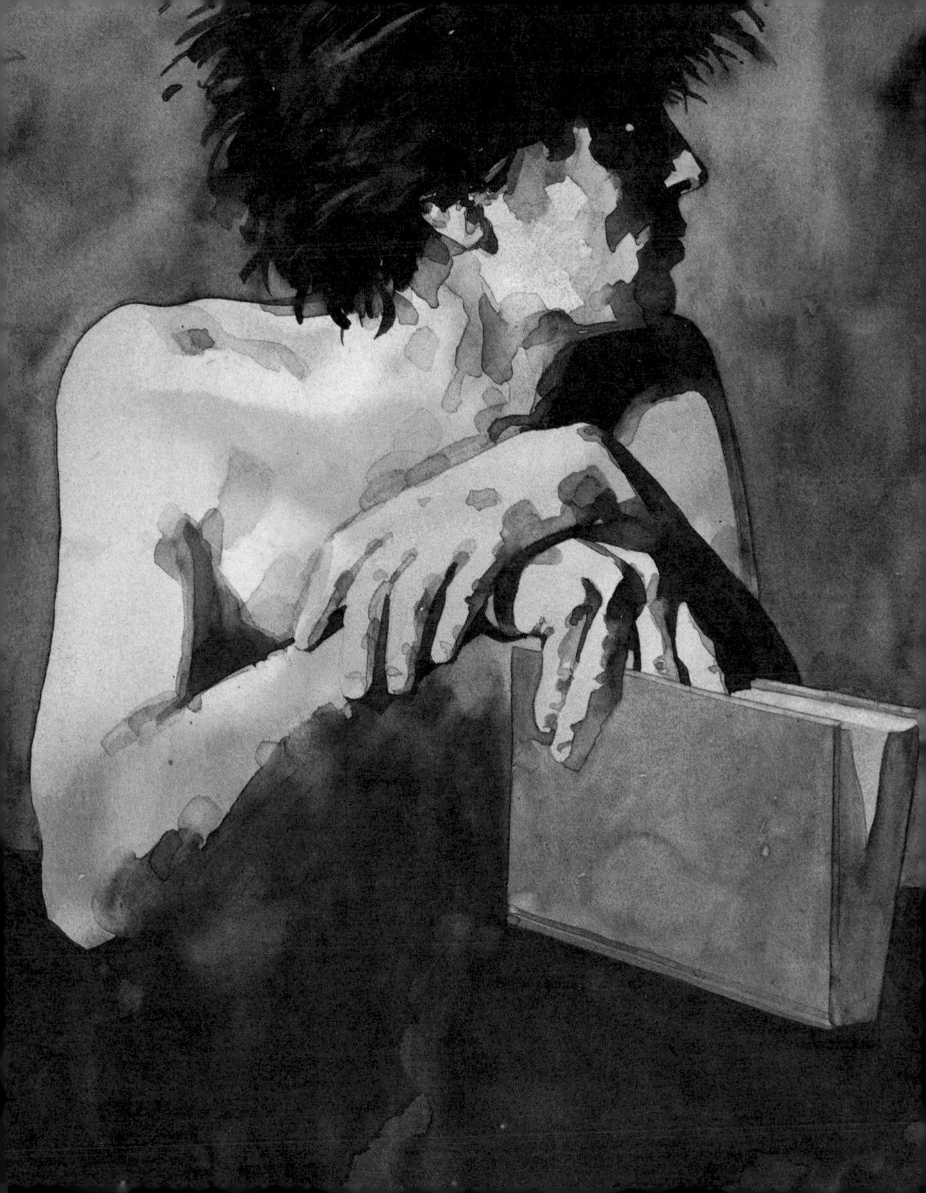

Mostly they aren't too keen to see me.

They fear the sunless lands.

But they enter your realm

each night without fear.

And I am far more terrible

than you, my sister.

— Death to Dream

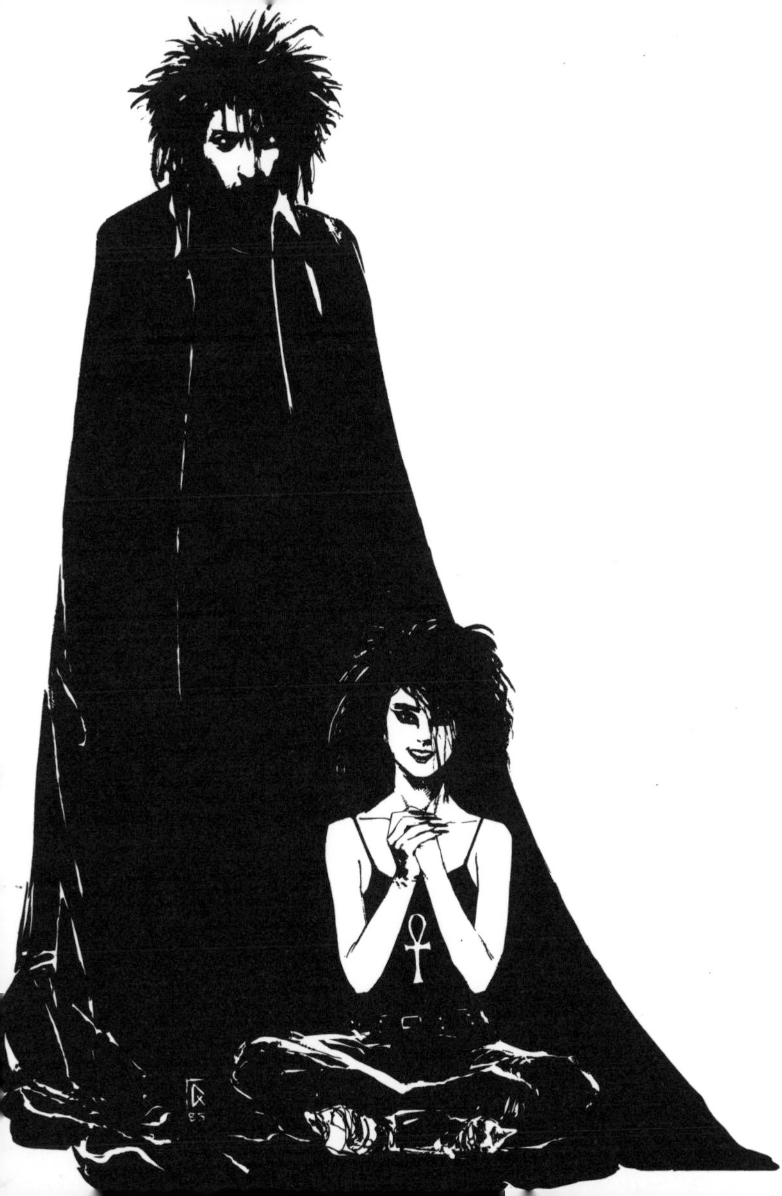

I'm not blessed, or merciful.

I'm just me.

I've got a job to do,

and I do it.

—Death

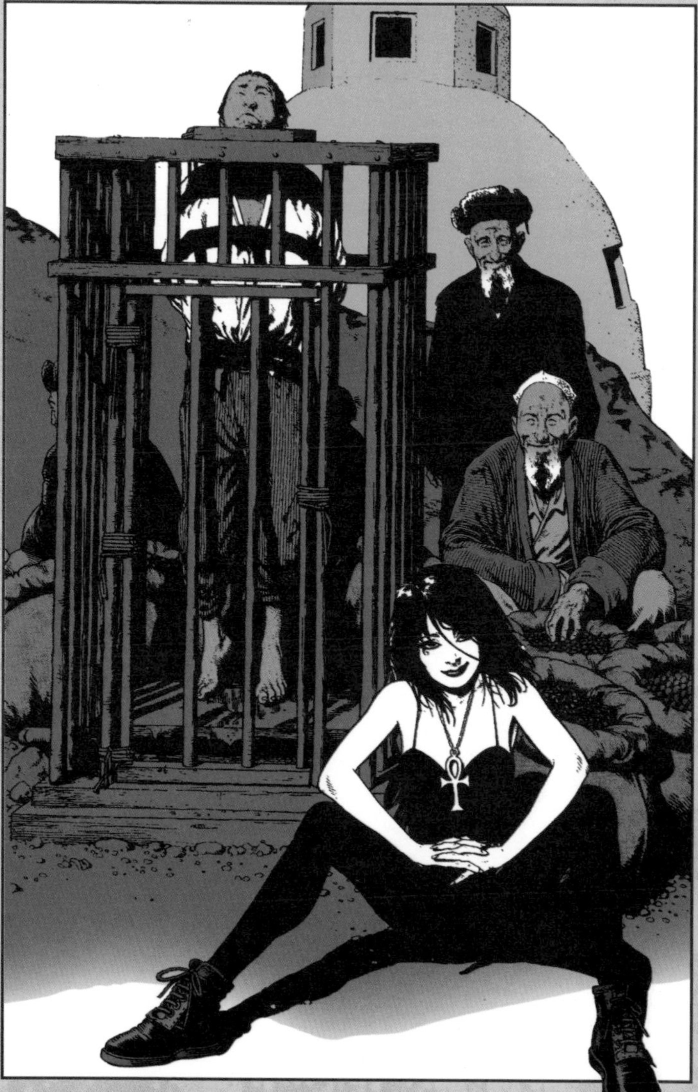

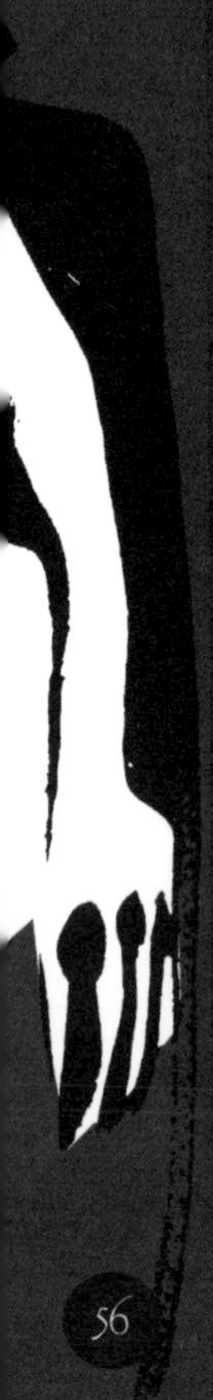

I don't know...Death's a funny thing. I used to think it was a big sudden thing, like a huge owl that would swoop down out of the night and carry you off. I don't anymore. I think it's a slow thing. Like a thief who comes to your house day after day, taking a little thing here and a little thing there, and one day you walk round the house and there's nothing there to keep you, nothing to make you want to stay.

And then you lie down
and shut up
forever.

— Hob Gadling

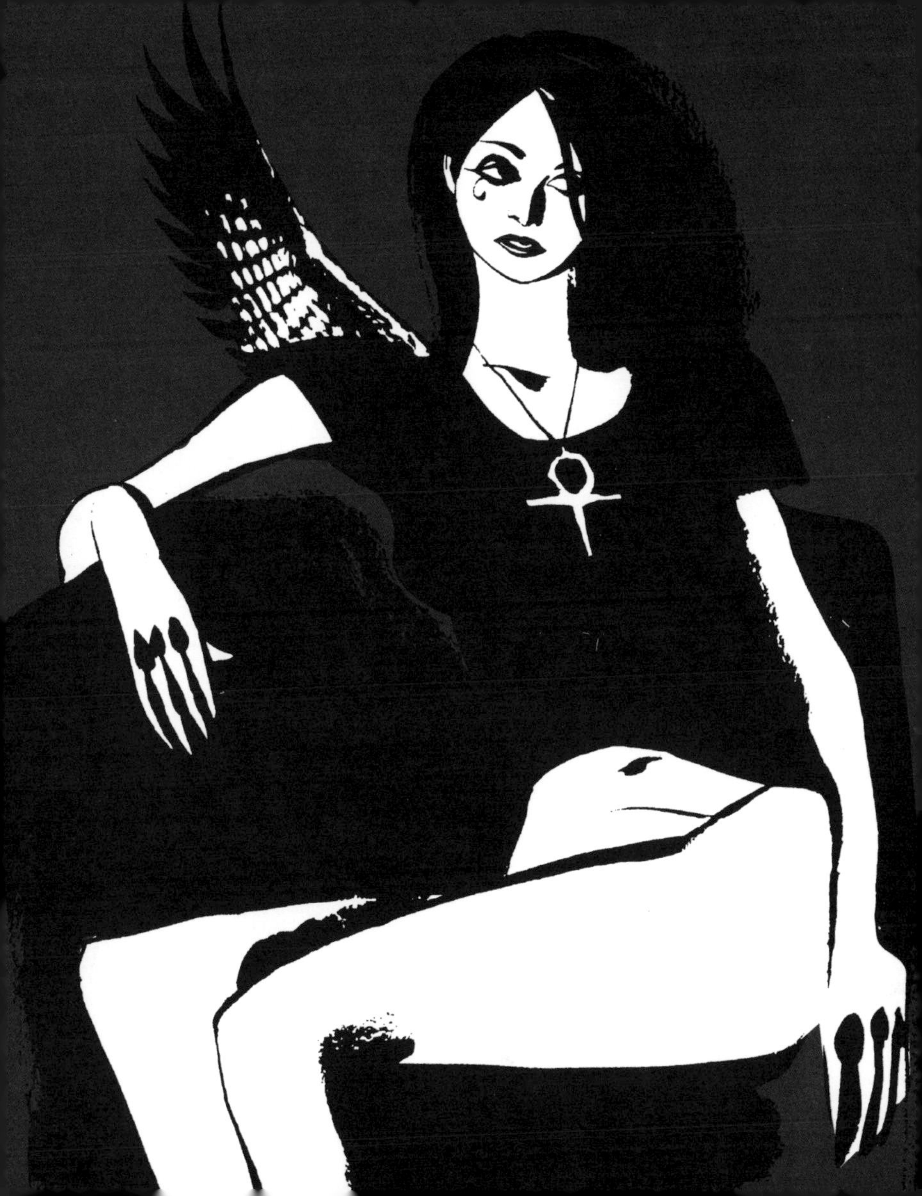

You got what anybody gets,
Bernie.
You got a lifetime.

—Death

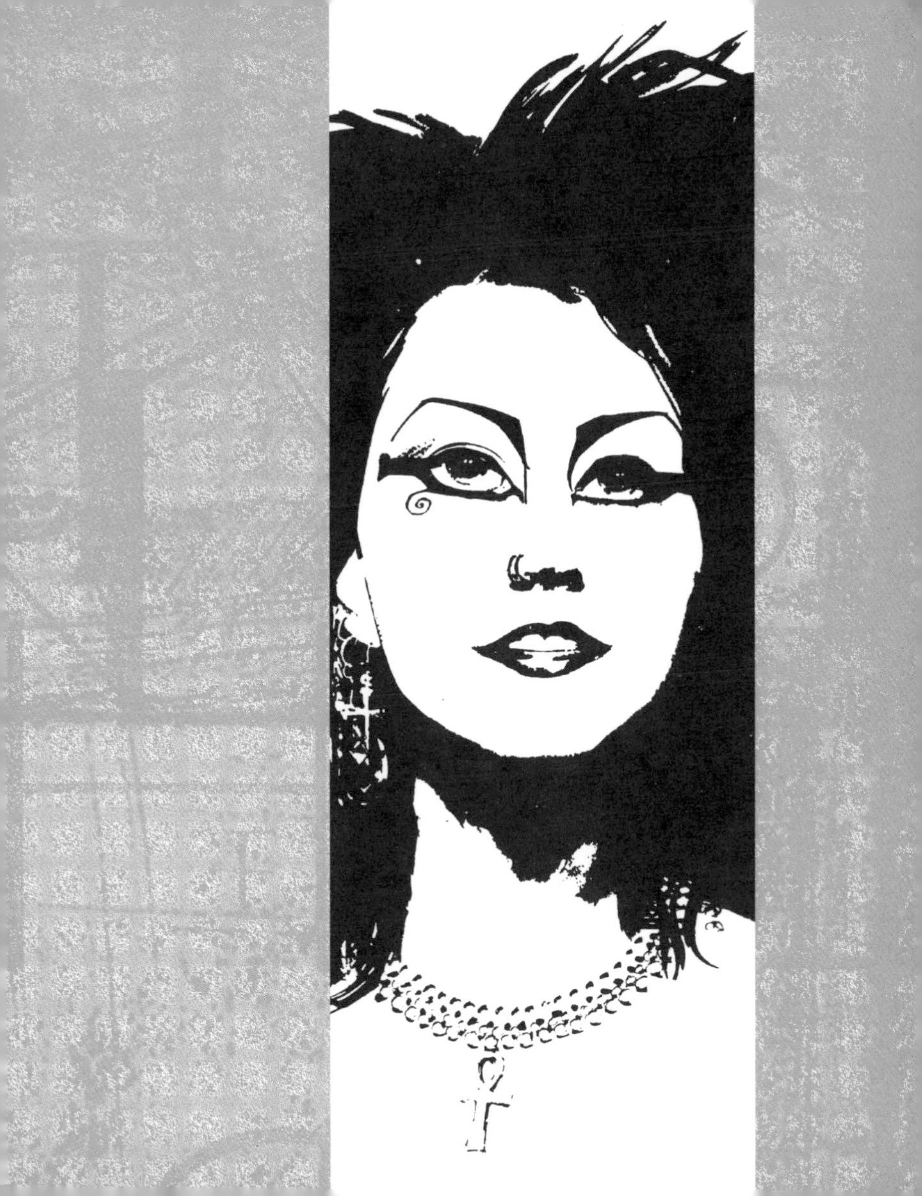

Have you ever been in love?
Horrible, isn't it?

It makes you so vulnerable. It opens your chest and it opens your heart and it means someone can get inside you and mess you up. You build up all these defenses. You build up this whole armor, for years, so nothing can hurt you, then one stupid person, no different from any other stupid person, wanders into your stupid life...You give them a piece of you. They don't ask for it. They do something dumb one day like kiss you, or smile at you, and your life isn't your own anymore. Love takes hostages. It gets inside you. It eats you out and leaves you crying in the darkness, so a simple phrase like "Maybe we should just be friends" or "How perceptive" turns into a glass splinter working its way into your heart.

It hurts. Not just in the imagination. Not just in the mind. It's a soul-hurt, a body-hurt, a real gets-inside-you-and-rips-you-apart pain. Nothing should be able to do that. Especially not love.

I hate love.

— Rose Walker

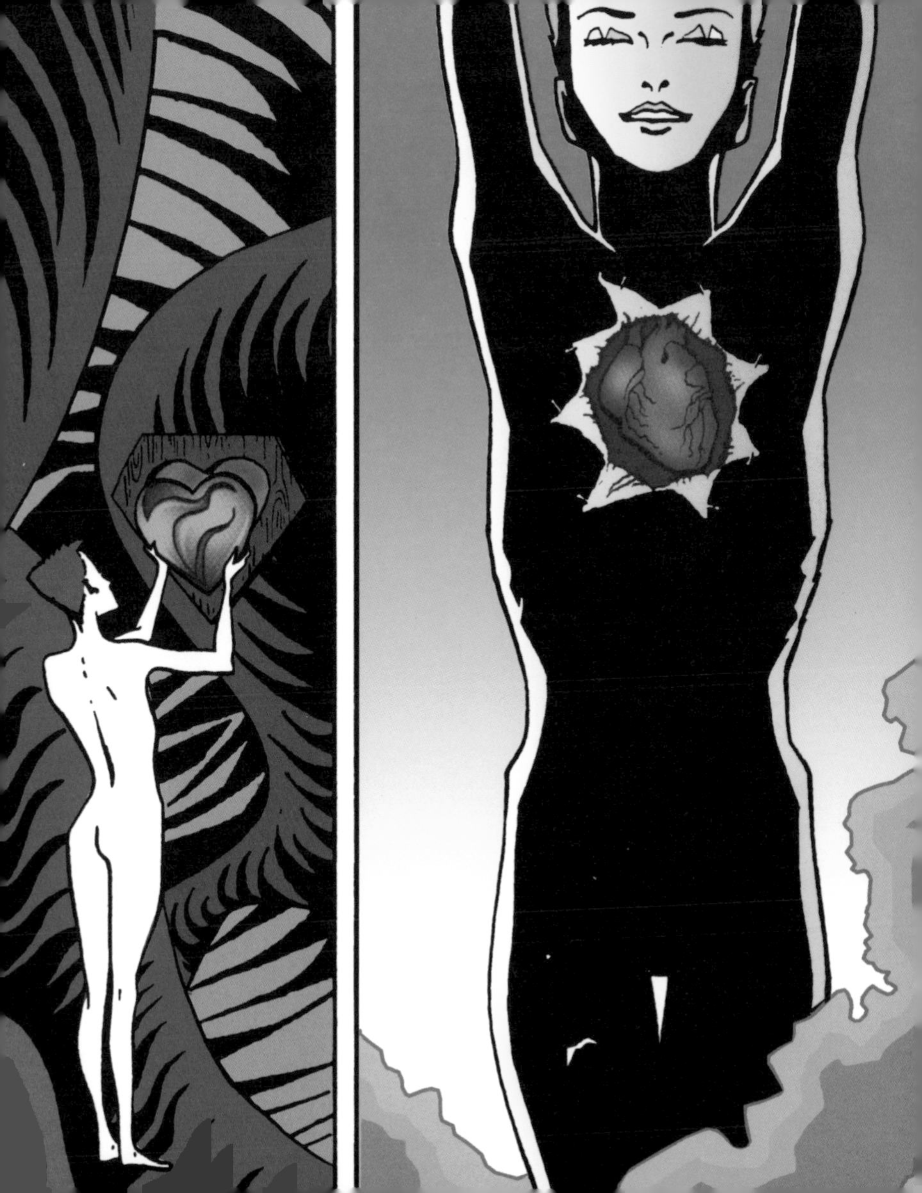

Love belongs
to Desire,
and Desire
is always
cruel.

— Old Man

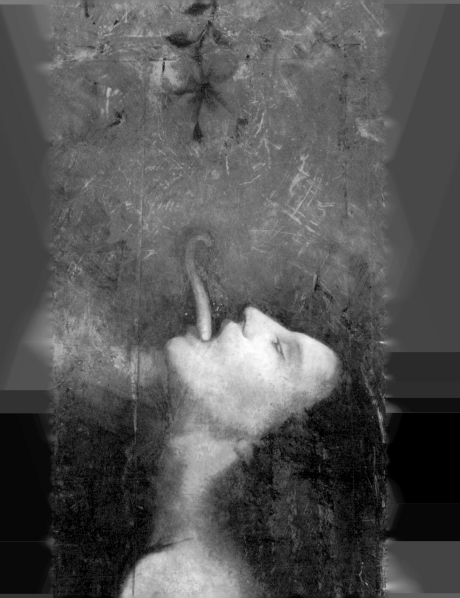

Me? Lady, I'm your worst nightmare —
a pumpkin with a gun.

— Mervyn Pumpkinhead

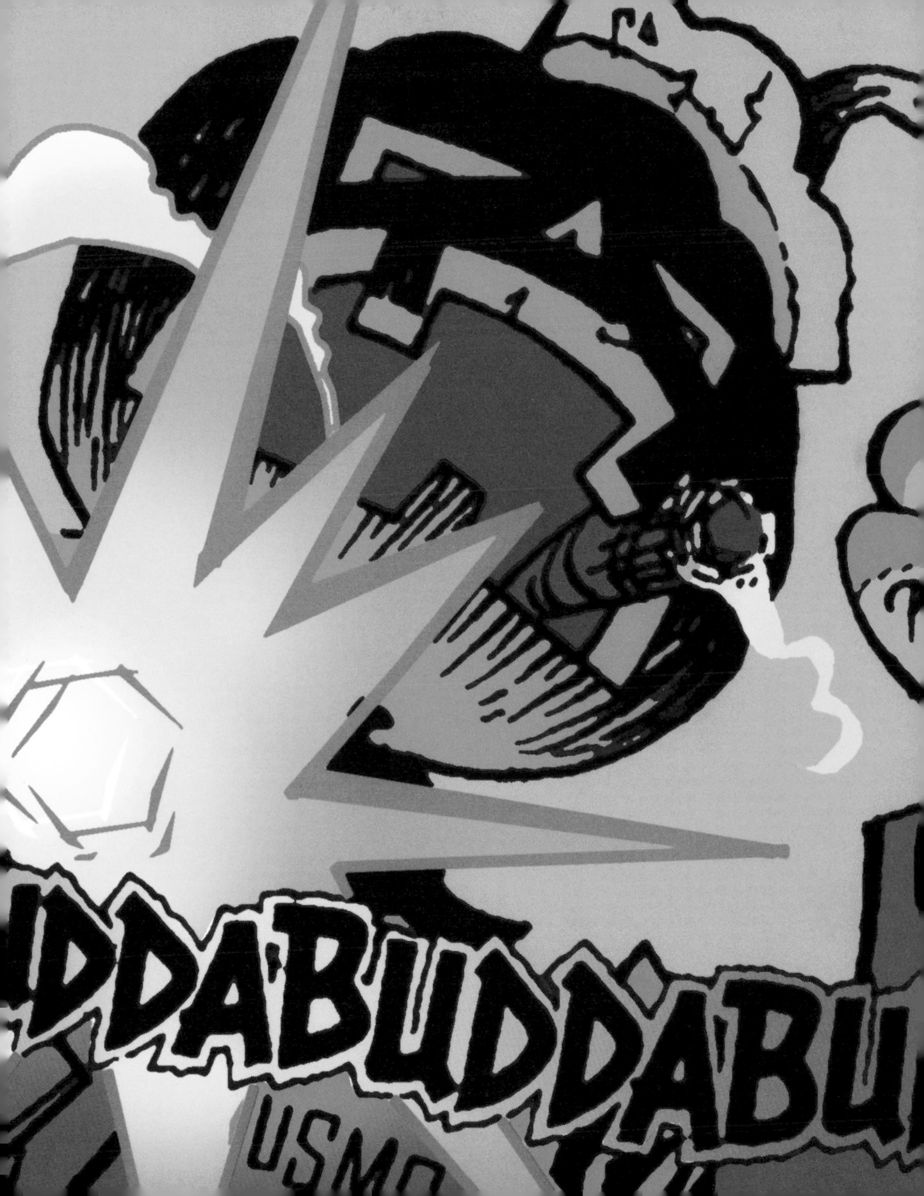
DDABUDDABU

Tools, of course,
can be the subtlest of traps.

— Daniel

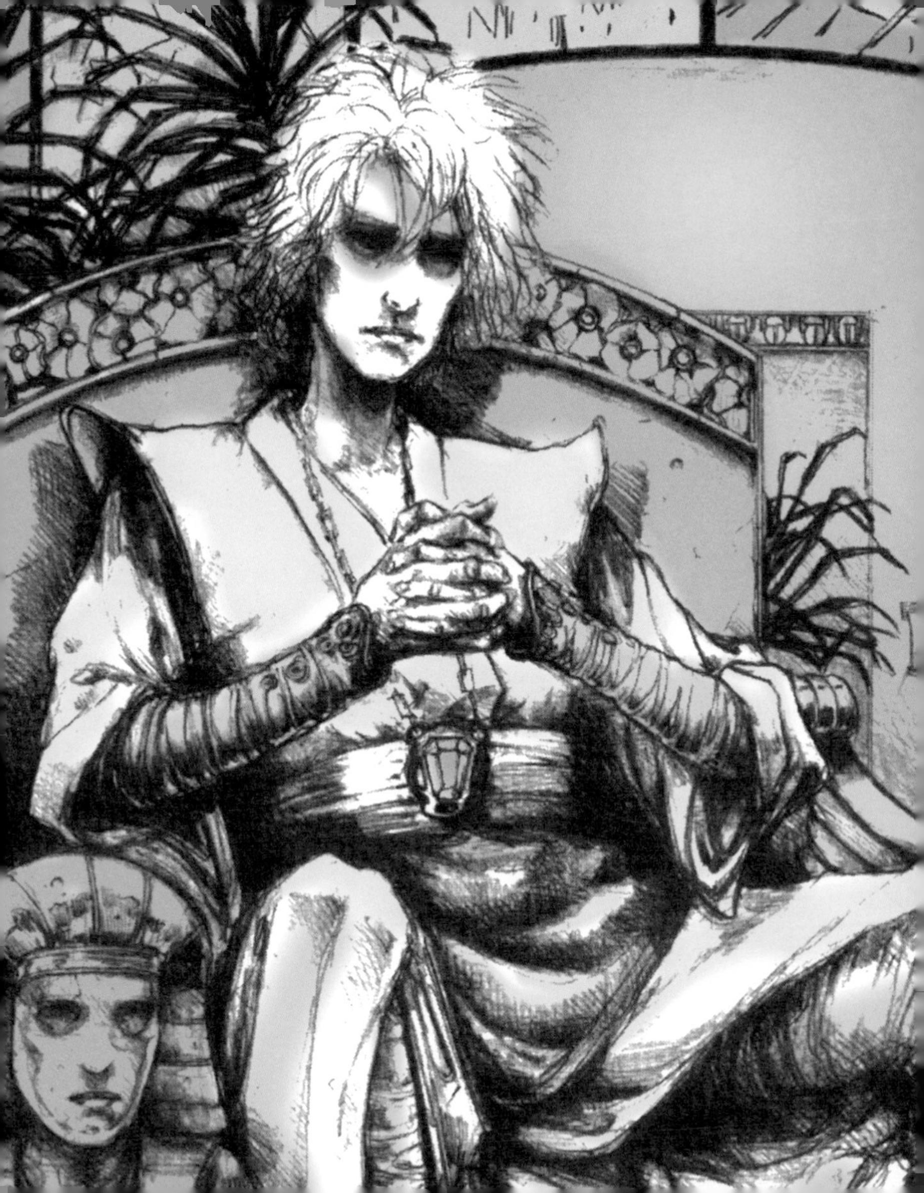

Charitably...
I think...
sometimes, perhaps,
one must change or die.

And, in the end, there were, perhaps,
limits to how much he could
let himself change.

— Lucien

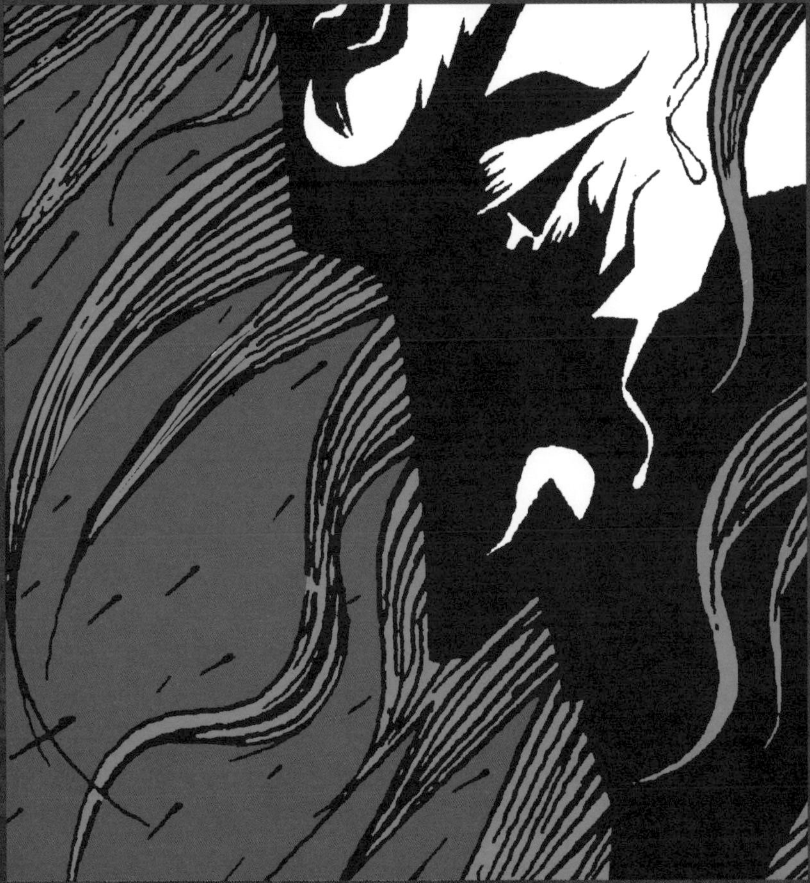

Only the phoenix arises and
does not change.
And everything changes. And
nothing is truly lost.

— Narrator

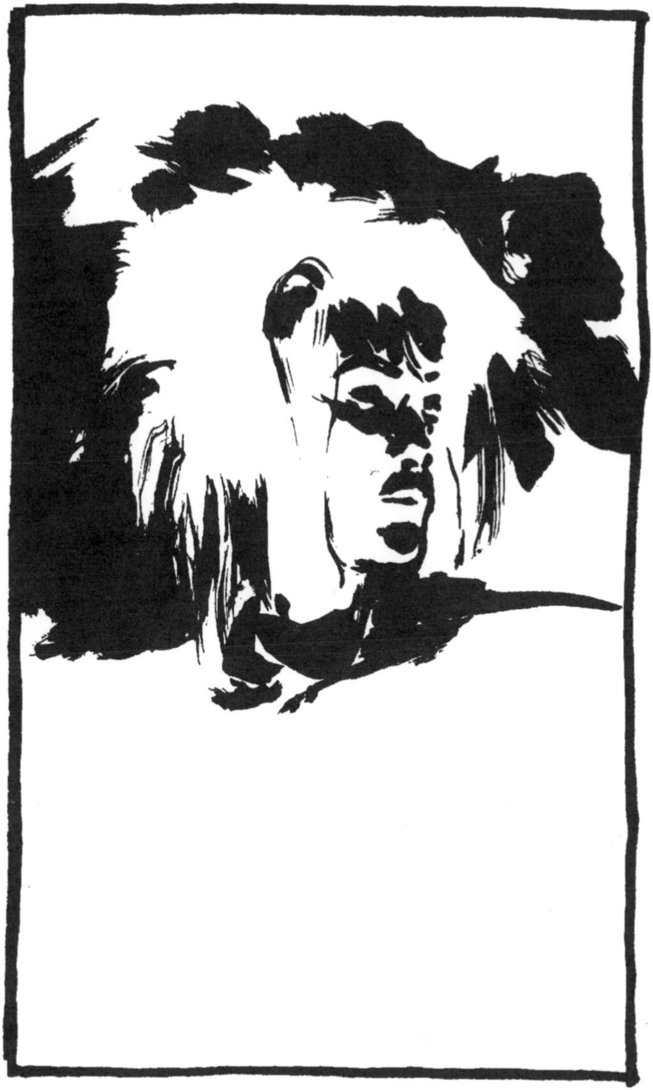

That which is dreamed
can never be lost,
can never be undreamed.

— Master Li

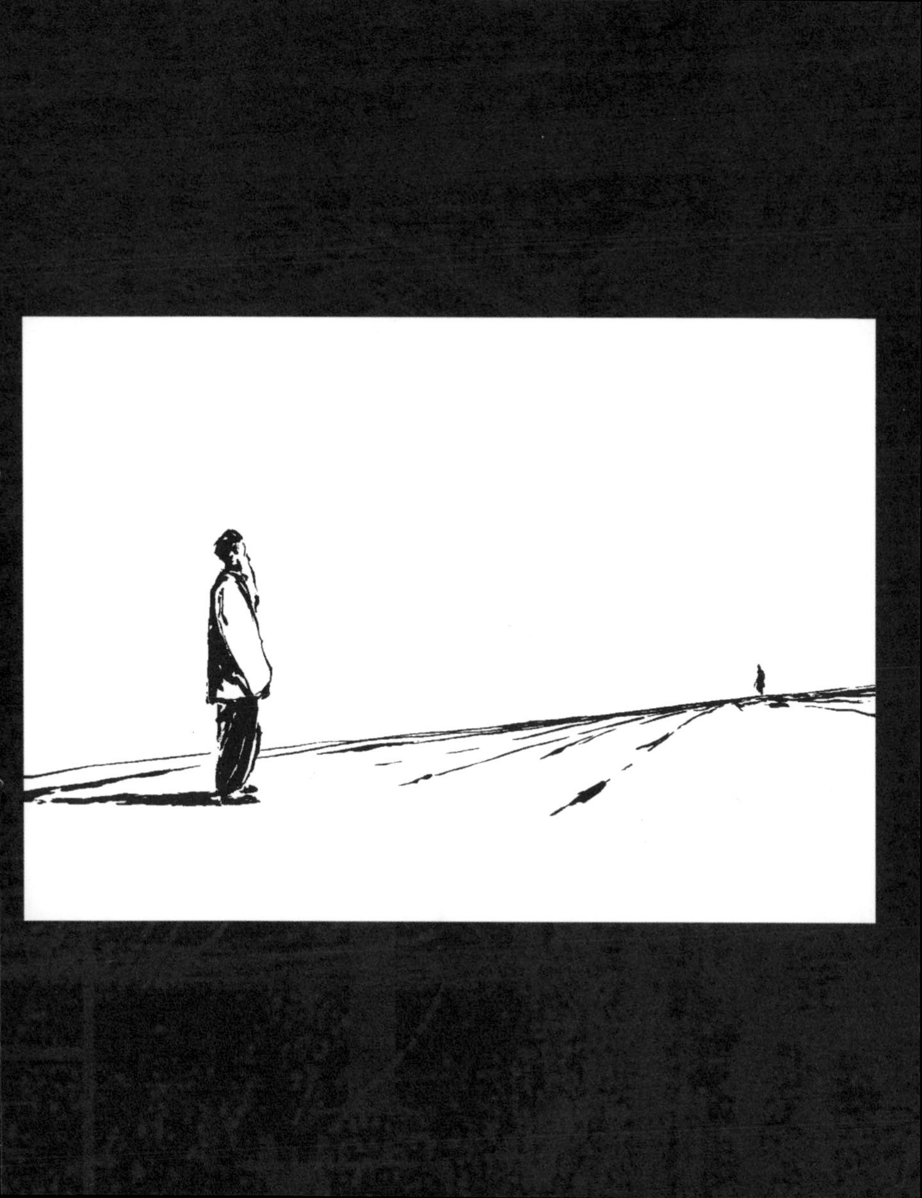

Nobody died. How can you kill an idea?
How can you kill the personification of an action?

Then what died? Who are you mourning?

A puh-point of view.

— Cain, Eblis O'Shaughnessy and Abel

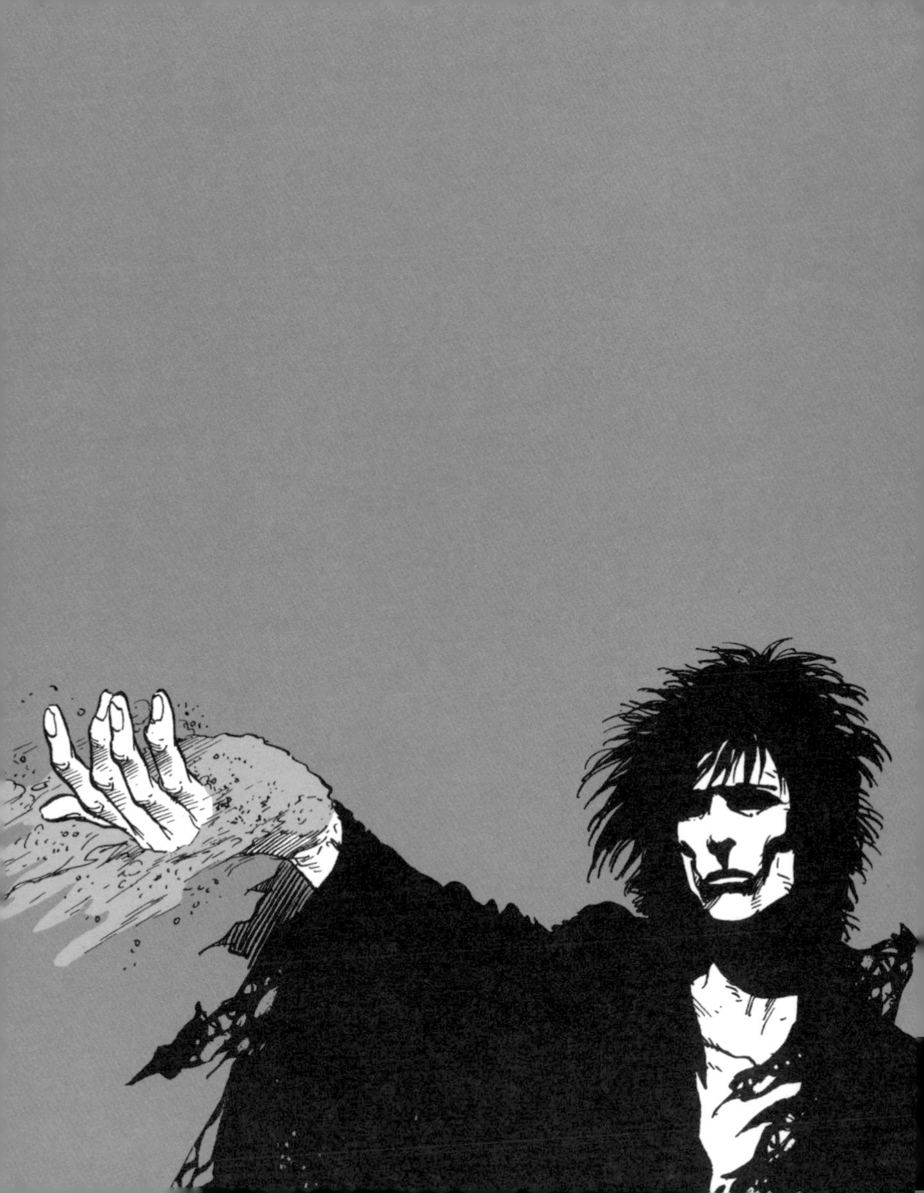

I know how gods begin, Roger. We start as dreams. Then we walk out of the dreams into the land. We are worshipped and loved, and take power to our-selves. And then one day there's no one left to worship us. And in the end, each little god and god-dess takes its last journey back into dreams, and what comes after, not even we know.

— Ishtar

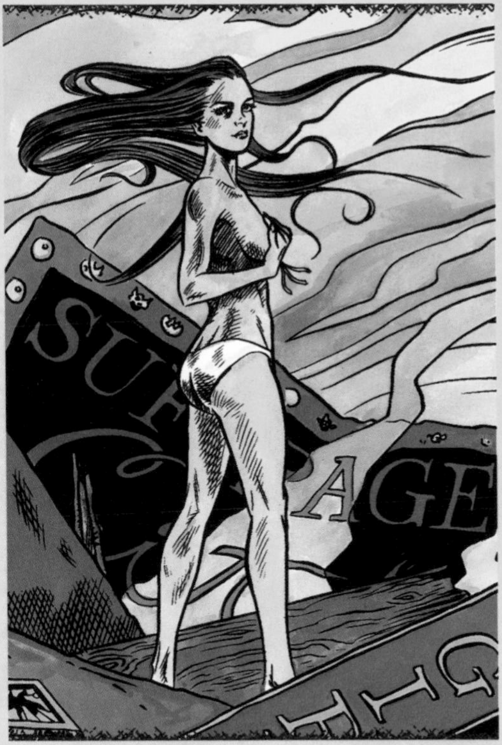
SUF
AGE

I like airplanes.
I like anywhere that isn't a proper place.

I like in-betweens.

— Delirium

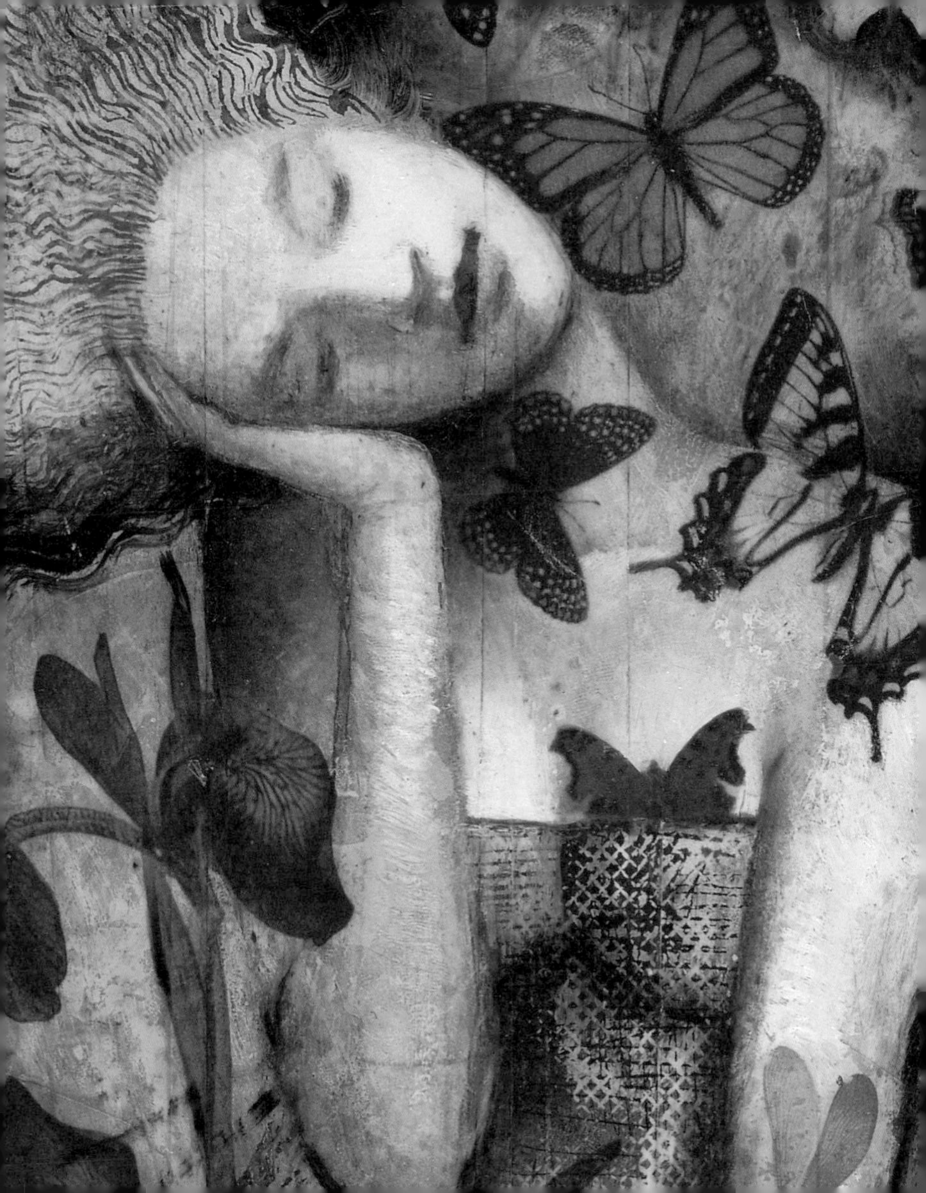

It has always been the prerogative of children and half-wits to point out that the emperor has no clothes.

But the half-wit remains a half-wit, and the emperor remains an emperor.

— Dream

I am following my fish.

— Delirium

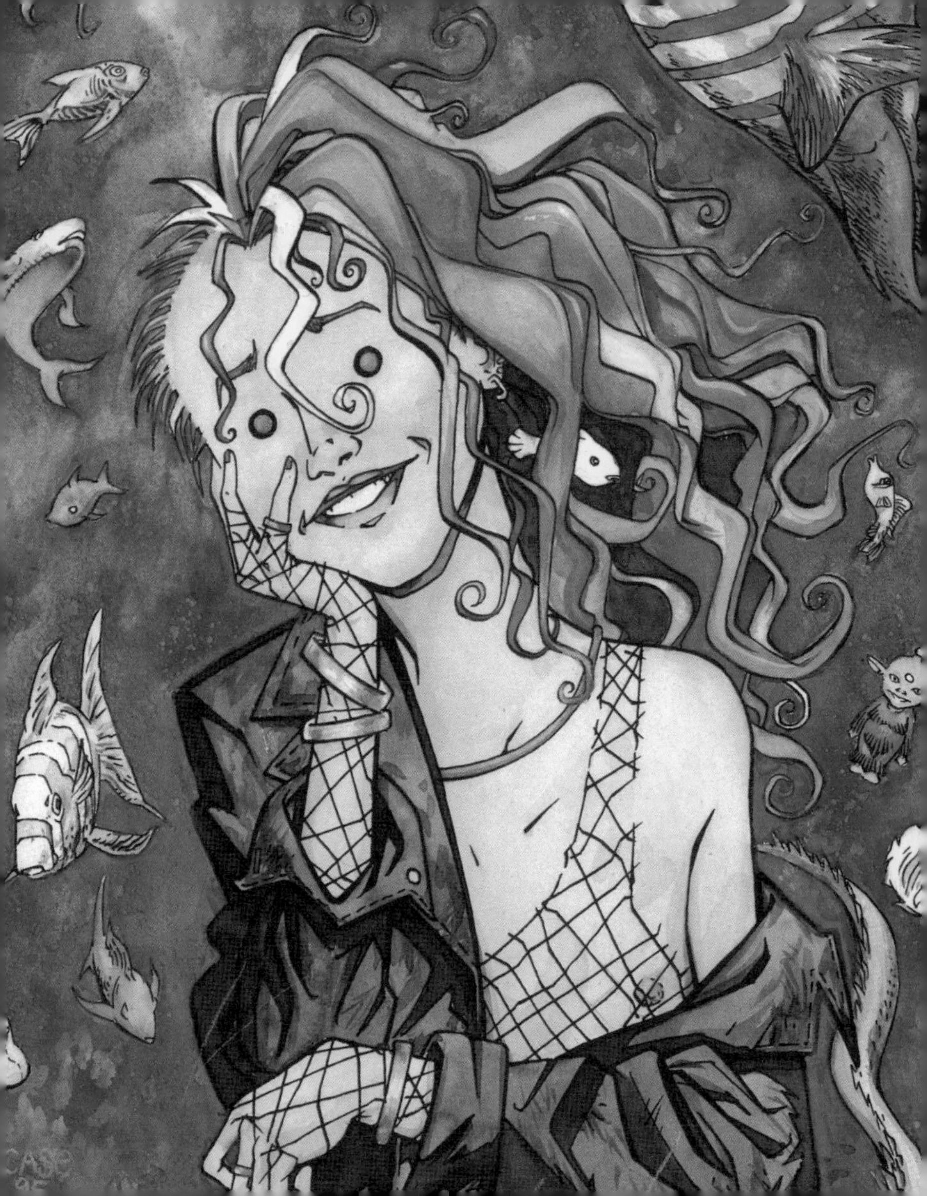
CASE

I loved bein' a kid. I was one of seventeen children. We were all named Wilkinson — I suppose it was roughest on the girls, but we all got used to it in the end. I blame the parents, really.

I would've liked to've bin an only child. That way when someone shouts Wilkinson, you know if it's you or not.

— Wilkinson

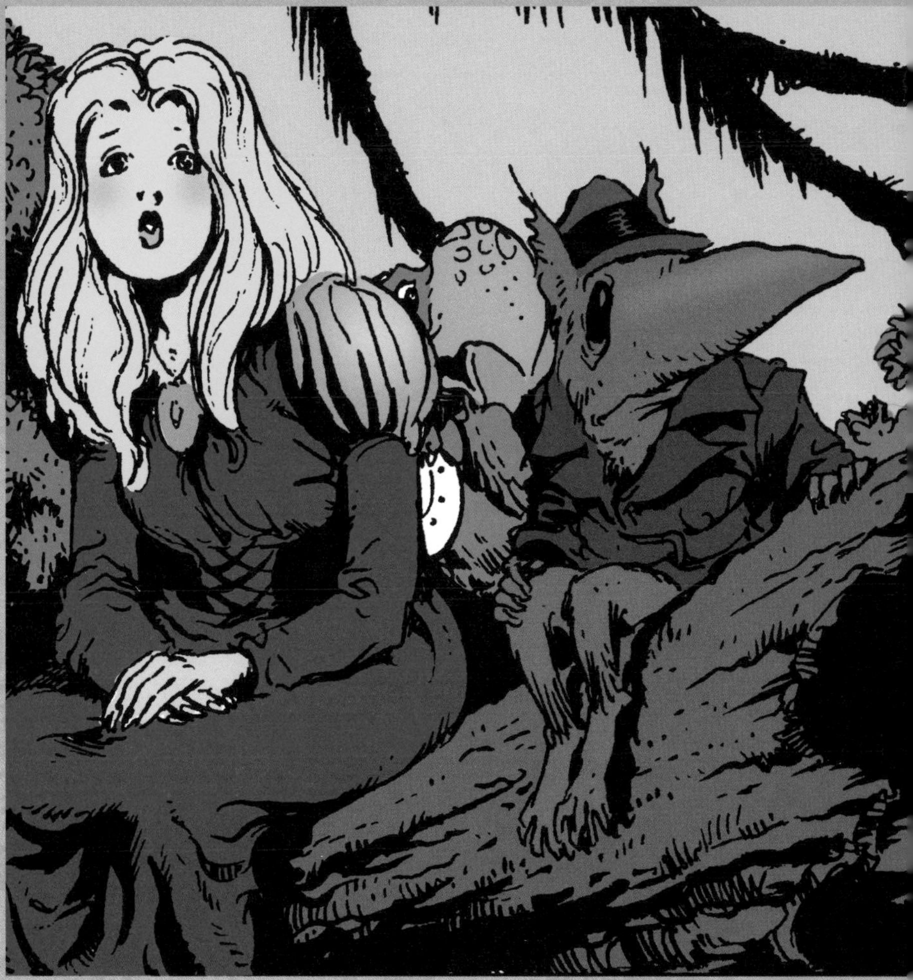

All Bette's stories have happy endings.

That's because she knows where to stop.

She's realized the real problem with stories —

if you keep them going long enough,

they always end in death.

— Narrator

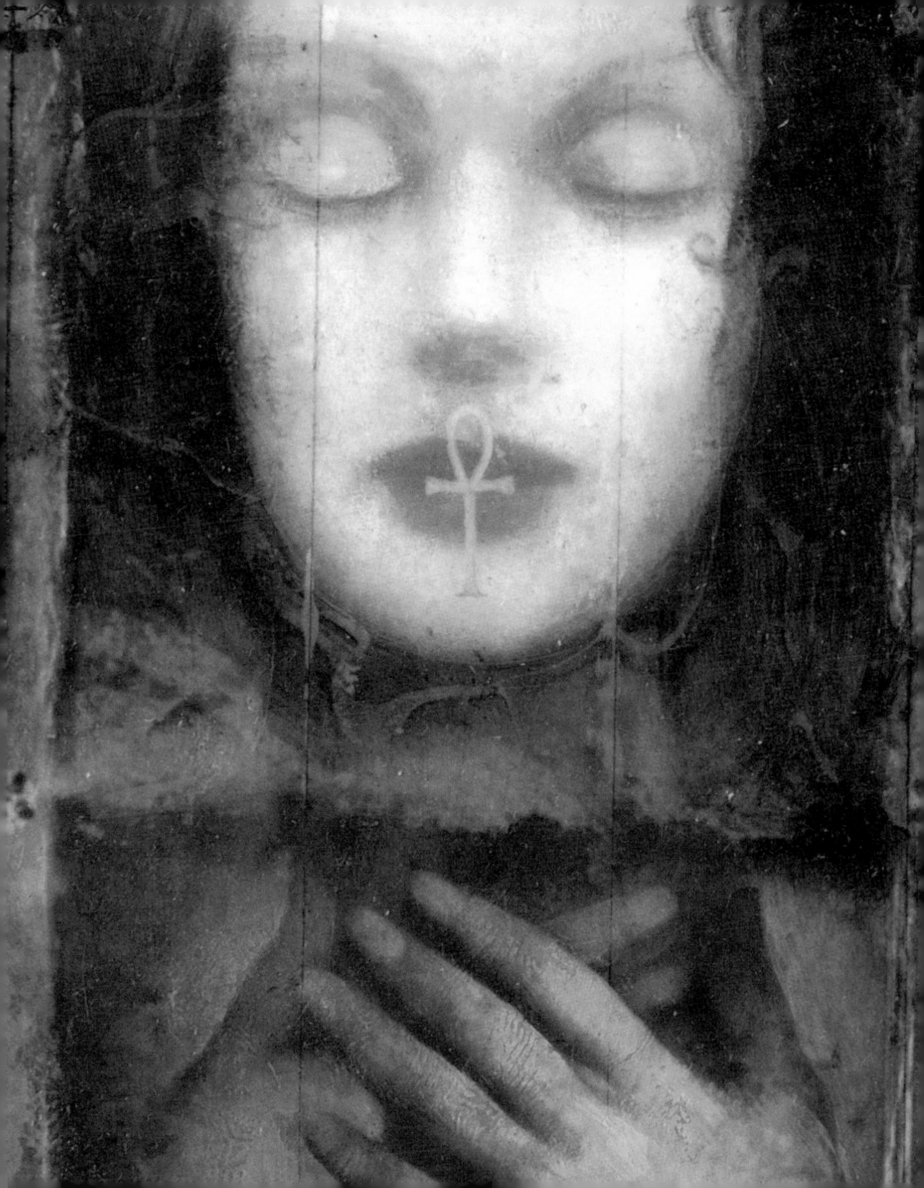

Can't say I've ever been too
fond of beginnings, myself.
Messy little things.
Give me a good ending any
time. You know where you are
with an ending.

— Crone

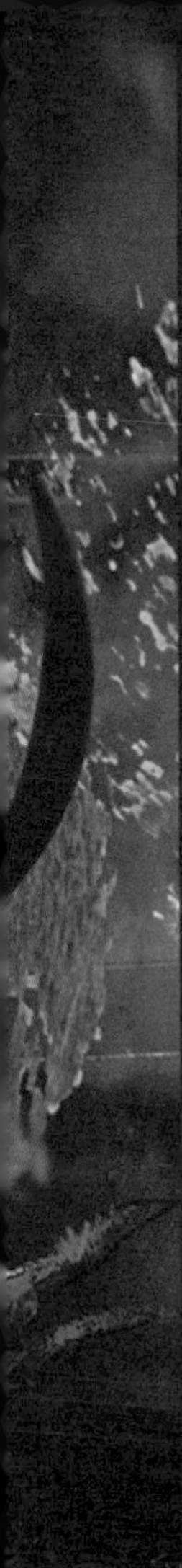

Well, there's only one way
to end a story, really.

Don't tell me: Happily ever after?

That's the one.

— Hob Gadling to Gwen

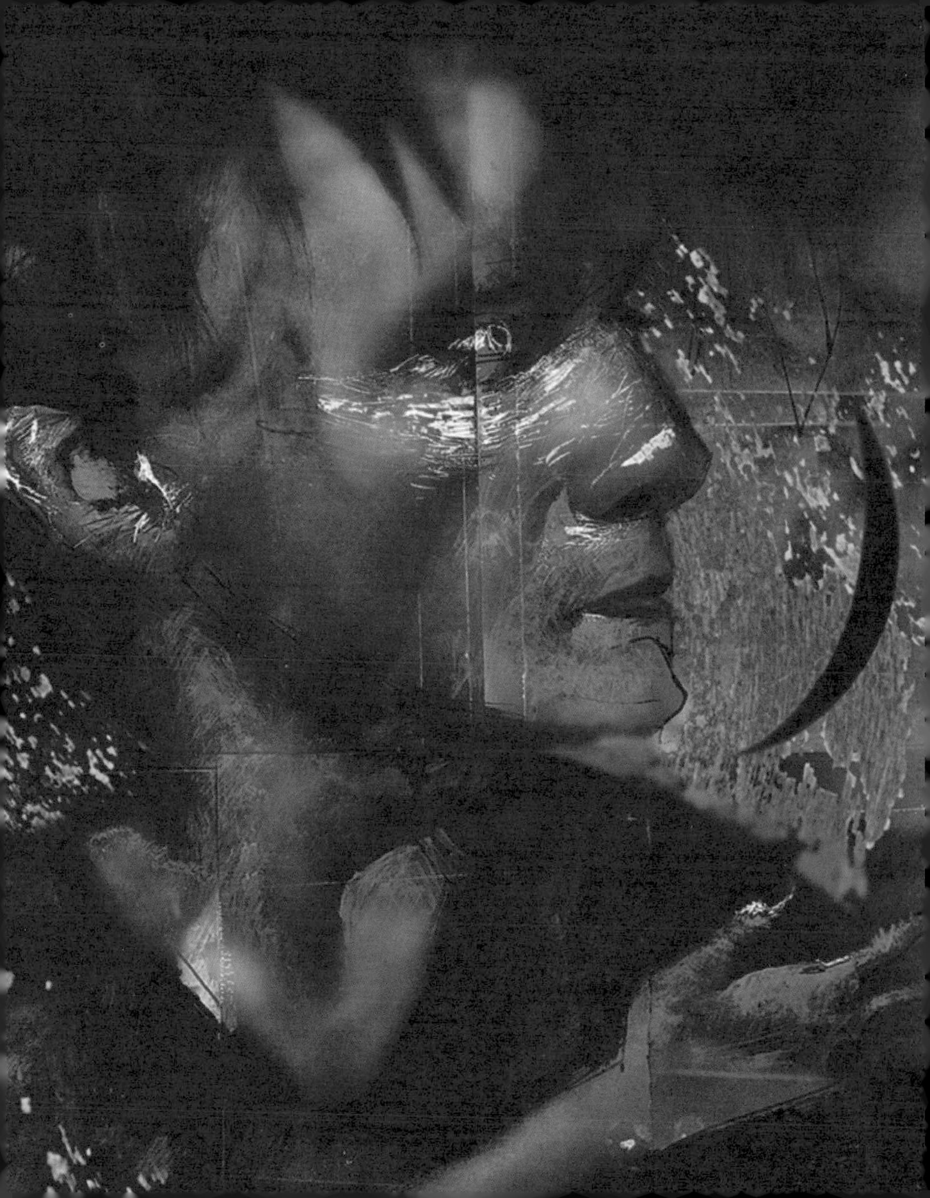

NEIL GAIMAN, WRITER
To set certain popular misconceptions to rest once and for all:

1) He was not found wandering the sewers of London as a child during the winter of 1864, unable to say anything more than "Powerful big rats, gentlemen."

2) He was never exhibited in public houses to the curious; only briefly in July, 1865, to selected gentlemen of standing from the scientific and literary community.

3) He did not have a vestigial tail.

4) He did indeed have what most people would commonly understand as "eyes."

5) He was not actually the pilot of the Zeppelin, although he did disappear for good following the explosion.

6) There is quite obviously no "underground kingdom beneath London inhabited by huge intelligent rodents." And even if there were, any suggestion of Neil's involvement in the mazy territorial negotiations between London's Above and Below can be considered a joke, and in poor taste at that.

7) He was afraid of neither mirrors nor street conjurers.

8) There were no tooth-marks on the bones.

"Writers are liars, my dear." — Erasmus Fry

Index of Quotations

p.2: DREAM COUNTRY, "A Midsummer Night's Dream," p. 21 panel 5

p.4: BRIEF LIVES, Chapter 3, p. 23 panel 6

p. 6: SEASON OF MISTS, Episode 0, p. 11 panel 1

p. 8: SEASON OF MISTS, Episode 1, p. 23 panels 1-2

p. 10: THE KINDLY ONES, Part 7, p. 1 panel 1

p. 12: FABLES & REFLECTIONS, "Fear of Falling," p. 6 panel 6, p. 10 panel 5

p. 14: THE DOLL'S HOUSE, Part 6, p. 22 panels 2-3

p. 16: THE WAKE, p. 13 panel 1

p. 18: BRIEF LIVES, Chapter 7, p. 15 panel 4

p. 20: WORLDS' END, "A Tale of Two Cities," p. 11 panel 6

p. 22: WORLDS' END, "A Tale of Two Cities," p. 18 panels 1-2, p. 23 panels 4-5

p. 24: DREAM COUNTRY, "A Midsummer Night's Dream," p. 6 panel 4

p. 26: PRELUDES & NOCTURNES, "The Sound of Her Wings," p. 9 panel 4

p. 28: SEASON OF MISTS, Episode 2, p. 18 panel 3

p. 30: DREAM COUNTRY, "A Dream of a Thousand Cats," p. 23 panel 3

p. 32: BRIEF LIVES, Chapter 1, p. 23 panel 3

p. 34: DREAM COUNTRY, "A Midsummer Night's Dream," p. 19 panel 3

p. 36: FABLES & REFLECTIONS, "The Song of Orpheus," p. 15 panels 4-6

p. 38: BRIEF LIVES, Chapter 8, pp. 2-3

p. 40: THE KINDLY ONES, Chapter 8, p. 8 panel 6

p. 42: THE KINDLY ONES, Part 11, p. 24 panel 4

p. 44: DREAM COUNTRY, "Façade," p. 20 panel 6

p. 46: BRIEF LIVES, Chapter 8, p. 16 panel 5

p. 48: SEASON OF MISTS, Episode 0, p. 9 panel 1

p. 50: BRIEF LIVES, Chapter 2, p. 5 panels 2-5

p. 52: PRELUDES & NOCTURNES, "The Sound of Her Wings," p. 17 panel 6

p. 54: DREAM COUNTRY, "Façade," p. 20 panel 2

p. 56: THE WAKE, p. 111, panels 6-8

p. 58: BRIEF LIVES, Chapter 3, p. 5 panel 2

p. 60: THE KINDLY ONES, Part 9, pp. 7-8 panels 4-9

p. 62: THE DOLL'S HOUSE, "Prologue: Tale in the Sand," p. 14 panel 5

p. 64: THE KINDLY ONES, Chapter 10, p. 16 panel 5

p. 66: THE WAKE, p. 141 panel 4

p. 68: THE WAKE, p. 59 panel 6

p. 70: THE WAKE, p. 144 panel 3

p. 72: THE WAKE, p. 143 panel 8

p. 74: THE WAKE, p. 44 panels 3-4

p. 76: BRIEF LIVES, Chapter 5, p. 20 panels 7-8

p. 78: BRIEF LIVES, Chapter 8, p. 4 panel 4

p. 80: THE KINDLY ONES, Chapter 4, p. 23 panel 4

p. 82: THE KINDLY ONES, Chapter 12, p. 7 panel 6

p. 84: A GAME OF YOU, Chapter 4, p. 13 panels 1-2

p. 86: PRELUDES & NOC-TURNES, "24 Hours," p. 4 panel 1

p. 88: THE KINDLY ONES, Part 1, p. 1 panel 6

p. 90: THE WAKE, p. 118 panel 5

p. 92: SEASON OF MISTS, biographies; DREAM COUNTRY, "Calliope," p. 7 panel 5

Index of Artists

Front/Back cover:
Dave McKean

p. 3: Dave McKean

p. 5: Matt Wagner

p. 7: Rebecca Guay

p. 9: George Pratt

p. 11: Kent Williams

p. 13: K. Williams

p. 15: Mike Dringenberg &
Malcolm Jones III

p. 17: Glenn Fabry

p. 19: Jill Thompson

p. 21: G. Pratt

p. 23: Alec Stephens

p. 25: M. Dringenberg &
M. Jones III

p. 27: J. Thompson &
Vince Locke

p. 29: D. McKean

p. 31: John Watkiss

p. 33: K. Williams

p. 35: Charles Vess

p. 37: J. Thompson &
V. Locke

p. 39: J. Thompson &
V. Locke

p. 41: Sherilyn
Van Valkenburgh

p. 43: J. Thompson

p. 45: Rick Berry

p. 47: Paul Lee

p. 49: R. Berry

p. 51: Mark Chiarello

p. 53: M. Dringenberg

p. 55: Brian Bolland

p. 57: D. McKean

p. 59: M. Dringenberg &
M. Jones III

p. 61: Marc Hempel &
D'Israeli

p. 63: Greg Spalenka

p. 65: M. Hempel &
Richard Case

p. 67: Michael Zulli

p. 69: M. Hempel

p. 71: Jon J Muth

p. 73: J. Muth

p. 75: Shawn McManus

p. 77: Michael Allred

p. 79: G. Spalenka

p. 81: Denys Cowan

p. 83: R. Case

p. 85: S. McManus

p. 87: G. Spalenka

p. 89: M. Zulli

p. 91: D. McKean

p. 92: Neil Gaiman